A PALMETTO CHRISTMAS

MILTON J. DAVIS

MVmedia, LLC
Fayetteville, Georgia

Copyright © 2024 by Milton J. Davis.

All rights reserved. No part of this publication may be reproduced, distributed, or transmitted in any form or by any means, including photocopying, recording, or other electronic or mechanical methods, without the prior written permission of the publisher, except in the case of brief quotations embodied in critical reviews and certain other noncommercial uses permitted by copyright law. For permission requests, write to the publisher, addressed "Attention: Permissions Coordinator," at the address below.

MVmedia, LLC
PO Box 143052
Fayetteville, GA 30214
www.mvmediaatl.com

Publisher's Note: This is a work of fiction. Names, characters, places, and incidents are a product of the author's imagination. Locales and public names are sometimes used for atmospheric purposes. Any resemblance to actual people, living or dead, or to businesses, companies, events, institutions, or locales is completely coincidental.

Book Layout ©2017 BookDesignTemplates.com
Cover Art by Amber Denise

Ordering Information:
Quantity sales. Special discounts are available on quantity purchases by corporations, associations, and others. For details, contact the "Special Sales Department" at the address above.

A Palmetto Christmas/ Milton J. Davis. -- 1st ed.
ISBN no.: 979-8-9905120-0-9

Contents

-1- 7
-2- 13
-3- 20
-4- 25
-5- 30
-6- 39
-7- 45
-8- 45
-9- 70
-10- 80
-11- 89
-12- 96
-13- 119
-14- 124
-15- 134
-16- 158
-17- 168
-18- 183
-19- 202

- 20 - 214
- 21 - 221
- 22 - 235

To Vickie.

Merry Christmas.

-1-

Laura Jacobs stared at the pile of yard tools blocking her Christmas ornaments and pitched a fit.

"Stanley! If you don't come in here and move all this junk off my Christmas decorations, I'm giving them all to Bob next door!"

Stanley opened the garage door then stuck his head out.

"As long as he pays for them," he said.

Laura picked up one of Stanley's work gloves then threw it at him. Stanley ducked inside and the glove bounced off the door.

"You make me sick," Laura said.

Stanley stepped into the garage and they both laughed.

"I'll move them out of the way," he said. "Though I don't see why we're going through all this. The kids and grandkids won't be here. It's just you and me."

"And we're not worth celebrating?" Laura asked.

"I didn't mean that. It's just a lot of work, and we ain't spring chickens anymore."

"I still want my Christmas decorations," Laura said.

Stanley's eyes went wide, and he smiled.

"Hey, remember how we always said we wanted to spend Christmas somewhere different?"

Laura's eyebrows rose and her smile matched his.

"Yes, I do."

"Let's do it this year," Stanley said.

"There's no reason why we shouldn't," Laura replied. "Nobody's coming."

Stanley folded his arms. "So, where do you want to go? Maine?"

"Shoot no!" Laura said. "I ain't never dreamed of a white Christmas."

"What about Sea Island?" Stanley suggested. "It won't be warm, but there won't be snow. We can take our own food and a few of our Christmas items to decorate the place."

"So, what are you waiting for?" Laura said. "Get on your computer and pull up Air B and C!"

"It's Air BnB, baby."

"Whatever. Get us a condo."

Laura followed Stanley through the kitchen then up the stairs to their office, which used to be Shelley's bedroom. A melancholy look came to her face as Stanley sat down before their desktop to log in. Her sigh caught his attention.

"You thinking about Baby Girl?"

Laura sat beside him.

"Yes, I am," she said. "At least she's out of Afghanistan."

"Still ain't home though."

"No, she isn't," Laura folded her arms across her chest. "I'm getting tired of this man's army."

"Cat will be okay," Stanley said. "She's the youngest and the toughest."

"Have you talked to Bryce lately?" Laura asked.

"Yeah," Stanley replied. "He's still looking for a job. I told him we could send him some money, but he refused. He said he's sure something will come up."

"I hope so," Laura said. "His savings is only going to last so long. I hate not seeing him, April, and the grandbabies."

"I hate they divorced," Stanley said. "He and April seemed like the perfect couple. She was a sweety, too."

"You never know what's going on between people, even your children. And you know how Bryce is. That boy won't talk about anything until he ain't got no choice."

"All we can do is pray and be ready to help," Stanley said.

"Amen."

"Anything from Terry?" Stanley asked.

"No."

Laura and Stanley fell silent. Terry was their wayward child. She was never happy at home, and once she finished college she left. She would call every now and then and occasionally visit, but her life was a mystery.

"Maybe she'll call this year," Laura finally said.

"Don't get your hopes up," Stanley replied.

"I always do. I'm a mother."

Stanley typed in the website then entered the dates for Christmas while Laura put on her reading glasses. They leaned in close to the screen, then reared back with scowls.

"You wouldn't think folks would be traveling on Christmas," Stanley said.

"I know, right?" Laura agreed. "The condos available are high, too."

"Well, so much for that idea," Stanley said.

"Wait a minute," Laura replied. "Let's look at the beach houses."

Stanley turned to look at Laura.

"Baby, if the condos are this high, the houses are gonna be crazy high. Besides, we don't need all that room. It's just you and me."

"We don't need it, but we always wanted it," Laura said. "A big ol' house right on the water? Looking out at the ocean while we eat our breakfast on the balcony?"

Stanley grinned. "That would be nice. Still, we can't afford it."

"Let's look anyway. What else we got to do?"

Stanley shrugged then pulled up the beach houses. Laura's eyes widened as she pointed at the screen.

"I love that one!"

They scrolled through the room pictures.

"This is perfect," Stanley said. "But look at the price."

"Let's talk to the owner," Laura replied.

"Why?"

"Maybe we can haggle with them."

Stanley rolled his eyes. "Here you go. This ain't no flea market, baby. These houses are expensive for a reason."

"We can try," Laura said. "What if it was you? Would you rather your house sits empty or make a little money?"

"That makes sense, but . . ."

"Call, baby. Let me talk to them."

Stanley shook his head and chuckled. "There you go with that smile when you want something."

"You gonna call them or what?"

Stanley picked up his cell and punched in the numbers.

"You got it on speaker?" Laura asked.

"Yeah."

The phone rang.

"Hello?" It was a woman's voice.

"Miss Appling?" Laura asked.

"Yes?"

"This is Laura Jacobs. How are you?"

"Excellent! And you can call me Judy."

"Well Judy, my husband and I are planning on visiting Sea Island for the holidays, and we're very interested in renting your home."

"Great choice!" Judy said. "I know you'll love it. The beach view from the master suite is amazing."

"I'm sure it is," Laura replied. "There's only one problem."

"Here we go," Stanley whispered.

Laura cut him a mean eye before continuing. "Well, your rates are kind of steep."

"This is a full house," Judy said. "We're talking six rooms and seven baths. And it's right on the beach."

"That's true, but I would think the rates would be lower due to it being off season."

"There really is no off season for Sea Island," Judy replied. "Lots of retirees and their families come to the island during the holidays."

"Let me ask you a question," Laura said. "Have you had any other offers for your house this season?"

"Actually, I haven't," Judy replied.

"And it's late in the season, too," Laura said. "It would be ashamed to have such a lovely place sitting empty like that, not making money."

"You do have a point," Judy said. "I might be able to drop the price a bit if you're willing to guarantee that you'll rent the property. I'll have to run it by my husband, but I think he'll go for it."

Laura winked at Stanley, and he rolled his eyes.

"Judy honey, if you can do that for me, we'll reserve it today."

"Let me get back with you," Judy said. "Is this a good number?"

"Yes, it is."

"I'll call you back in a few."

Laura disconnected. She looked at Stanley with a wide grin.

"I should have bet you money," she said.

Stanley shrugged and walked away.

"I don't see why. It's your money, too."

Laura laughed then threw a couch pillow at him. "You're welcome."

-2-

US Army Captain Shelly Jacobs inspected her makeup and black midi dress one last time before grabbing her purse. She was happy to be out of uniform and looking forward to hanging out with her friends at the local club in downtown Frankfurt. A twinge of sadness snuck through her usual good mood. Another Christmas would be spent in Germany instead of home. There was one good thing that would come out of it; the care package Mama would send would be amazing as it always was.

She stuck her head in Charlotte's room. Known for her precision and punctuality on base, the petite bundle of energy from Mobile, Alabama shed that persona with her uniform when it was time to hang out with her girl.

"You ready?" Shelly asked out of habit.

"Almost!" Charlotte yelled from her bathroom.

Shelly shook her head, then strolled into the kitchen and grabbed a box of crackers from the cabinet. She turned on the TV then plopped onto the couch to nibble and chill.

Five minutes later the bathroom door opened, and Charlotte emerged like a high fashion model on a runway. The red mini hit all the right notes, and her jewelry sparkled even in their uneven light.

"You don't have to say it," she said. "I know I look good."

"I wasn't going to say that," Shelly replied. "Let's go, with your pretty late ass."

They laughed as they left their apartment and clambered down the stairs to the parking lot. The snow from the previous day had been shoveled away and cleared from the cars. Shelly loved their complex maintenance, despite the rent being a bit steep for her salary. The perks made it worth it.

They climbed in her white BMW then set off.

"Is Damian going to be there?" Charlotte asked.

"I don't know," Shelly replied. "I haven't heard from him in a while."

Shelly glanced at Charlotte. "Not that you care anyway."

"I don't," Charlotte confessed. "I'm just hoping if he is, he'll bring his fine ass friend with him."

"If he's there, Javan will be there. They're inseparable like us."

"Well hurry up," Charlotte said. "Can't keep them boys waiting for all this." She swept her hand along her body.

"Girl, you are crazy," Shelly said. She pressed the gas.

The Indigo Blue was a jazz spot frequented by American military and local Germans. Shelly wasn't a big jazz fan, but it was a nice chill spot with good drinks and a great vibe. It was also an excellent place to meet 'grown' men. Charlotte took her to the club one weekend when she was feeling sorry for herself. Though she and Sam had broken up two years ago, there were still times when it felt like yesterday. They were in love; well, at least she was, and his announcement that he could no longer deal with their long-distance relationship stunned her. She suspected there was someone else, but she was too hurt to argue.

She met Damian a year later, and they'd been seeing each other off and on ever since. Though they enjoyed each other's company, the relationship had yet to move beyond flirting. They both were holding back for their own reasons. For Shelly, it was fear. For him, it was something else. Tonight, she was determined to find out. Their flirtation had reached a turning point. It was either grow or go.

They entered the club and were greeted by relaxing music and admiring stares.

"There they are!" Charlotte said.

Damian and Javan sat at their usual table, drinks in hand. They raised them in unison. Charlotte led the way, weaving through the tables like an athlete on an obstacle course. Shelly took her time, her eyes locked on Damian. She enjoyed the way he looked at her, like he was enjoying everything he saw. She would give him all the time he needed.

Both men stood then pulled the two empty chairs at the table away for them to sit. Old school gentlemen, she thought. It reminded her of how Daddy treated Mama, and there was comfort in that.

"We're the luckiest men in Blue Indigo," Javan said.

"You say that every time," Charlotte replied.

"And I mean it every time," Javan said.

Shelly placed her hand on the table and Damian covered it with his.

"Hi," he said.

Shelly smiled. "Hey."

The waiter came to their table and the ladies ordered their drinks.

"Put it on my tab," Javan said.

Everyone at the table leaned back in mock shock.

"Javan? Paying?" Damian said. "I hope y'all prayed up. The world is about to end."

Javan's joy dimmed a bit. He gazed at Charlotte and his smiled brightened.

"Care to dance?" he asked.

"Yes!" she said.

Javan extended his hand and Charlotte took it. Together they walked in time with the music to the modest dance floor. Shelly watched them for a moment then turned back to Damian.

"You want to dance?" he asked.

Shelly shook her head. "I'm not much of a dancer. I'm that one Black person the dance gene skipped."

"You just haven't danced with the right person," Damian said.

"That's good. That's really good. But I need to ask you a question."

Damian squeezed her hand. "What is it?"

"Damian, what are we doing? I like you, and I feel like you like me. But I can't go on just feelings. I need to know."

Damian scooted his chair closer to her.

"Shelly, I've been crazy about you since day one. The only reason I didn't say anything earlier is because I sensed you weren't ready for a serious relationship."

"Oh, so you're psychic?"

Damian laughed. "No! It was the way you were around me. Like you were holding back."

"I was," Shelly confessed. "I was in a serious relationship that didn't end well. It's been two years, but it still hurts. I wasn't interested in dealing with anyone until I met you. Which excites me and scares me at the same time."

"Look Shelly, I don't know what's going to happen in the future with us. Let's just take it one day at a time for now, okay?"

Shelly felt a nervous rumble in her stomach. She didn't know if she could handle one day at a time. She could see herself falling hard for Damian, and if things didn't work out, she could feel that pain all over again. She knew what she had to do. She decided to change the subject.

"So, what are your Christmas plans?"

Damian looked confused for a moment, then smirked.

"I'm on leave starting next week," he said.

"That's a lot of time. I guess you'll be heading back to the States then."

Damian shifted in his seat.

"Actually no. I plan on traveling to Switzerland or France. Or maybe Spain."

Shelly's eyebrows rose. "I'd thought you would want to be with family this time of year."

"Not really," he replied. "That's the last place I want to be."

She squeezed his hand. "Anything you want to talk about?"

"No," Damian said. "It's complicated."

Damian stared into his glass, a blank look on his face. He raised his head with a smile.

"How about you? What are your plans?"

Shelly sighed. "Another Christmas in the Fatherland."

"Well since we're both going to be here, maybe we could travel together."

"Look, Damian, maybe we should . . ."

"Woo chile!"

Shelly looked up to see Charlotte and Javan standing behind her.

"This man dances like Usher!"

"What you talking about, Ciara?" Javan replied.

They laughed then sat down. Shelly was grateful for the interruption.

"Why y'all come back to the table lying like that?" Damian said.

17

Javan laughed. "Excuse me, hater. Have you seen my friend Damian?"

Javan ordered another round of drinks. He downed his quickly then cleared his throat.

"I have something to tell y'all," he said. "Yesterday I learned I'm being promoted to vice president of operations for my company."

"Congratulations!" Charlotte said. She raised her glass, and the others did the same.

"So, when do you start?" Damian asked.

Javan looked nervous. "Beginning of the year, after I move back to the States."

Charlotte's face drooped. Damian looked shocked, and Shelly was suddenly sad for her girlfriend.

"Move back to the States?" Charlotte said.

Javan's face turned serious. "Yeah. I was in Germany to oversee European operations. My new job puts me in charge of the globe."

"You can do that from anywhere, can't you?" Charlotte asked. Shelly heard the desperation in Charlotte's voice. This was about to get embarrassing.

"I could, but the powers that be won't let me. At least not right now. So, I'm relocating to Atlanta."

Charlotte stood. "Javan, can I talk to you in private?"

"Ah, yeah."

Javan stood and they walked away. Damian and Shelly sat in silence, sipping their drinks. Shelly avoided Damian's questioning gaze. She couldn't believe she was breaking up with him before they even started dating. The thought made her giggle; she looked up and Damian was looking at her with hope. She was about to say something when Javan and Charlotte returned.

"We're leaving," Charlotte said.

"Wait, what?" Shelly replied.

"We're leaving," Charlotte repeated. "We only have a month, so there's no time to waste. Don't wait up, Shelly. I'll be just fine."

Javan shrugged, a silly look on his face.

"See y'all whenever bruh," he said.

Javan extended his arm. Charlotte took it and they hurried away.

Damian finished his drink. "Well, that was something."

"It sure was," Shelly said. She stood then put on her coat. "I better be going."

"Please don't," Damian said. "I was hoping we could talk a little bit. Figure things out, maybe?"

"I don't think I'm ready, Damain," Shelly forced herself to say.

"So, you won't see me anymore?"

Shelly was quiet. She knew she was hurting him, but she also felt that falling in love with him might hurt her more.

"I don't know," she said.

She turned and hurried away before he could say another word.

-3-

Bryce was washing dishes when his phone erupted with *The Peabodys* cartoon theme music. He glanced at the screen.

"Daddy, we're here!"

Bryce dried his hands with the flowered hand towel Mama gave him years ago before making his way to the garage. He shut off the alarm then hit the button to open the garage door. The bright LED lights from April's SUV blinded him for a minute, but when his eyes cleared his children were bounding toward him, backpacks bouncing off their backs.

They said in unison.

Cameron hugged his leg while he swept Constance into his arms. There was a break in the light and April walked into the garage. Bryce's smile faded. He put Constance down.

"Y'all go on inside and put your stuff away," Bryce said. "I'll be in in a minute."

The children ran inside. Bryce folded his arms across his chest. April smiled, and he felt his heart lurch.

"Hi, Bryce."

"What do you want?" he replied.

April dropped her head and sighed.

"I'm not here to fight," she said. "I just wanted to ask if you're okay."

"Why wouldn't I be?"

"I saw the news," April replied. "And unless I missed something, you're no longer employed."

"Why would you care?" Bryce said, struggling to maintain a tough exterior.

April's smile faded. "Because I should. Anything that affects you affects our children."

"It's a temporary setback," Bryce said. "I'll be okay."

"Don't lie to me," April replied. "Positions like that are rare, especially for a Black man."

"Look, I said I'll be fine," Bryce said. "Don't worry about me now. You never have before."

"Hold up," April said. "Don't act like I did something wrong to you. We agreed on this together."

Bryce didn't reply. He only agreed on a divorce because he knew she wanted it and he knew she was cheating on him. Again. He didn't want her to be anywhere she didn't want to be. Counseling wasn't working, and both of them didn't want the children to grow up in a broken home. The truth? Despite everything, he still loved her.

"That's right, we did," he finally said. "Thank you for bringing the kids over. I'll call if they forgot something."

"Bryce, you can hold off on the child support payments if you need to," April said.

"I'm good. I have enough saved up."

"That's my Bryce," April said. "Always prepared for the worst."

"Not always," Bryce replied.

He turned to walk away, but April grabbed his shoulder. He closed his eyes as he remembered her touching him in better times. When she still loved him.

"Look Bryce, I still care about you," she said. "Let me be nice to you."

Bryce turned to face her. He took her hand off his shoulder.

"Do what you want to do," Bryce said. "Just don't expect me to do the same. Goodbye."

"Bye," April replied.

Bryce went into the house. He stood still as he listened to April start the car then drive away. He went to the family room; the kids were playing a video game.

"Daddy, is dinner ready?" Cameron asked without looking away from the screen.

"I'm ordering pizza tonight," Bryce said.

"Yay!" the kids cheered.

Bryce called for a delivery then sat down with the kids and watched them play. The days tussling with them were gone; video games were much more interesting and challenging. Still, it was great to have them for the holidays. He scraped every spare dollar together to make sure he was able to get them great gifts. But that meant no trip to Mama and Daddy's house this year. They would do the best they could in Chicago.

His phone buzzed and he checked the screen. It was Mama.

"Hey, Mama."

"Hey, Baby."

The kids froze.

"Grandma!" Constance shouted. "I wanna speak to her!"

Bryce smiled as he stood then turned away.

"Let Daddy talk to her first," he said.

Constance sat hard, folding her arms across her chest then poking out her bottom lip.

"Okay," she grumbled.

"I'm back," he said.

"You got the babies?"

"Yes, ma'am."

"They with you the entire break?"

"Just until Christmas. I'll take them back to their mother on the 26th."

"How is April?"
"She's fine."
"Tell her I said hey."
Bryce was quiet for a minute. Mama was crazy about April. So was Daddy. He shouldn't get mad for her asking; they didn't divorce her, he did. And she was still the mother of their grandchildren. But he felt a little betrayed whenever they asked about her.
"Mama, I got to go."
"Okay, Bryce. I wish you could come down."
"Not this year. Maybe next year."
"Okay, Baby. Me and your Daddy are praying for you."
"Thank you, Mama. Tell Daddy I said hey."
"I will. Love you, Son."
"Love you, too."
Bryce smiled at his daughter. "Okay, Constance. You can talk to Grandma now."
He gave her the phone. He wished he could go home too, if just for a break. Mama and Daddy would steal the kids from him and he would just walk through the old neighborhood, thinking about what used to be. He felt a tug on his shirt then looked down into Contance's eyes.
"Here you to, Daddy." Bryce took his phone from Constance then put it in his pocket.
"Come play," she said.
Those two words melted the tension. He picked her up and hugged her. She giggled.
"Daddy! You're squishing me!"
He put her down then strolled across the carpet to her game controls.
"Alright Cameron, you ready for this whupping?"
Cameron rolled his eyes. "You wish, Old Man."

Bryce feigned shock. "Old Man? Let the button mashing butt whupping begin!"

A Palmetto Christmas

-4-

Terry watched the snow fall from the gray Banff sky. Her latest painting sat unfinished on the wooden easel, missing the perfect light that graced it on clear days. She listened to João banter with his older brother, Pierre. Their word sparring usually didn't bother her, but today felt different. She slipped into old memories, when she and Shelly did the same thing, playfully insulting each other until they got on Mama's nerves.

"That's enough," Mama would say. "Folks would think y'all hated each other talking like that."

She stretched then ambled into the bathroom and took a shower. When she emerged wrapped in a towel, João was off the phone.

"How's your brother?" she asked.

"Crazy as always," he replied. "He wants us to meet him in São Paulo for Christmas."

"I don't want to go to Brazil this year," Terry said.

João walked up to her and hugged her.

"Why not? It'll be fun."

"I'm not in the mood."

João shrugged then let her go. He skipped into the bathroom then closed the door. She waited until she heard the shower before slipping into a pair of old jeans and sweatshirt. She picked up her phone, scrolling through her contacts until she found Shelly's number. She thought about texting, but she wanted to hear her sister's voice. The phone buzzed.

"Terry!" Shelly answered.

A warm sensation flowed through Terry as she smiled.

"Hey, Little Sister," she said.

"Call me back on video," Shelly said. "I want to see you."

"Wait why?"

"Because I haven't seen you in three years!"

Terry let out a heavy breath. She hung up then called again, this time with video. Shelly's bright face appeared, and Terry was glad Shelly made her do it.

"Oooh, I like your hair! You went natural!" Shelly said.

"You know I always loved a good 'fro. And look at you with the braids. The army getting slack?"

"New year new rules," Shelly said. "So, where you at?"

"Banff," Terry said.

"Where?"

"Banff. Google it."

Shelly fell silent and Terry frowned.

"I didn't mean right now!"

Shelly laughed. "Ooh, nice! Kinda cold, ain't it?"

"That's how I like it in winter. João wants to go to Brazil."

"Who is João?"

"A friend."

"A fine friend?"

Terry laughed. Shelly always had a way of lightening her mood. Nothing was serious to her unless it was very serious. That feeling she'd suppressed earlier flared.

"A fine boyfriend," Terry said. She texted Shelly a photo.

"Deeeeem! Does he have a twin?"

"Shut up," Terry said. "Don't let Sam hear you say that."

The phone went quiet.

"Shelly?"

"There is no Sam," Shelly said, her voice flat.

"I'm sorry," Terry replied.

"Don't be," Shelly said. "Things happen."

"When did this happen?"

"Two years ago. If you answered a sistah's texts every now and then, you'd be up to date."

Terry hadn't talked to Shelly in years, but she knew that tone. It was time to change the subject.

"How's Bryce?"

"That's more bad news," Shelly said. "He and April divorced three years ago."

The news caught Terry off guard.

"Divorced? That's impossible! I never knew two people more in love!"

"Well again, shit happens," Shelly said. She didn't seem to be upset, but to Shelly Bryce could do no wrong.

"I hate to hear that. April was sweet."

"She's something, but Bryce is our brother, remember?"

"I know, but . . ."

"Terry, you should come home," Shelly said.

"I've been thinking about it," she replied.

"Stop thinking and do it," Shelly said. "It's been three years. I miss you; Bryce misses you; Mama and Daddy miss you."

"I don't believe the last two even notice."

"I'm not going to talk about that," Shelly said. "Just come home."

"Like I said, I'll think about it."

João came out of the bathroom shirtless in his underwear, drying his hair.

"I'll talk to you later," Terry said. "Bye."

She hung up.

"Who was that?" João asked. "Your petit co-pain?"

"My sister," Terry said.

João's eyes widened.

"So, you're speaking to your family again! Excellent!"

"João, I think I might want to go home for Christmas," Terry said. "You don't mind, do you?"

João shuffled to the bed then dropped beside her before wrapping his arms around her and kissing her forehead.

"Mind? I think it's wonderful!"

Terry smiled as she pushed him away.

"I can go home, and you can go to Brazil and meet your brother."

"Nonsense!" he said. "I see Pierre all the time, but I've never met your family. We can leave tomorrow!"

"Slow down!" Terry said. "We have a lot to do between now and then. And who's paying for this?" Terry asked.

"I am!" João replied.

"I can't ask you to do that," Terry said.

"You don't need to. I insist!"

Terry shrugged and smiled "Well in that case . . ."

"Great! Let me handle everything. By this time tomorrow we'll be landing in . . . where exactly do your parents live?"

"Atlanta."

"Atlanta!"

João jumped off the bed the ran to the dresser to get his phone. Terry watched him as a knot formed in her stomach. She was going home. She had no idea what to expect.

A Palmetto Christmas

-5-

No matter how many times they made the journey, the effect was still the same. Laura and Stanley listened to their Christmas playlist as the miles streamed by, the landscape gradually transforming from hilly hardwood piedmont to flat, pine covered sandy plains. They took their breaks at their usual spots, refreshing and refueling, their anticipation growing. As they reached the intersection of I-16 and I-95, their excitement was obvious. They were almost there.

"So, what you want to do?" Stanley asked. "Take 95 north straight to the island or stop in Savannah for a few?"

"Let's head to the island," Laura said. "But let's drive through Savannah. I like the scenic route."

"That's because you ain't been driving for four hours," Stanley said.

Laura kissed him on the cheek. "You don't mind, Baby. Do you?"

Stanley smiled as he followed I-16 until it vanished into Savannah. They drove through the city then crossed the high arc bridge spanning the Savannah River, descending into South Carolina. The road narrowed from four to two lanes bordered by lives oaks and swatches of marshland. When they began visiting over twenty years ago this stretch of road was mostly empty, the natural vistas occasionally interrupted by a lone home or trailer park. Now the span was mostly developed, the beauty diminished but not eliminated.

They finally merged onto the four-lane highway leading to Sea Island. This too had changed. Just like the backroads, the highway was bordered by restaurants, hotels, car dealerships, shopping centers and other monuments of progress. The old signposts signaling their nearness to the island had disappeared, all except the open-air seafood market at the base of the access bridge to the island. Laura would usually get Stanley to stop for fresh shrimp, but it was closed as would be expected this time of year.

As Stanley drove across the island bridge, Laura peered out of the window. Below them, the channel separating Sea Island from the mainland shimmered, with marshland from the mainland shores reaching out to the beach borders of the island. Majestic homes with personal docks were visible from the bridge's crest. Laura spotted a fishing boat in the distance, heading for open water.

"We're here!" Stanley said.

"Yes, we are!" Laura replied.

It didn't take long to get to their destination, Palmetto Marsh Resort. They stopped at the rental office for their parking pass then took their time driving down the narrow tree lined streets to their temporary home. The resort was adorned for the season as only Sea Island could do, lights strung on canal bridges, bike paths, and golf cart roads and spiraling up the palmetto tree trunks. The friendly woman at the security checkpoint for the beachfront homes waved them through, and they took a left to the road leading to their temporary paradise.

"Here we are," Stanley said.

He took a right down a narrow street and drove into a small cul-de-sac. In the center of the circle was their rental, all two-stories and four thousand square feet of it.

"Oh, my goodness!" Laura said. "It's huge!"

Stanley steered into the driveway and Laura jumped out of the SUV before he shut off the engine.

"Where you going?" he called out. "We have to get the luggage!"

"I want to see first!" Laura called out. "Come on!"

Stanley grabbed a suitcase before following Laura to the entrance. She entered the code, opened the door, and they stepped inside.

Laura and Stanley stood frozen in the massive granite floor foyer. The walls towered over them, with a magnificent chandelier so high it could only be reached with scaffolding. The entryway opened into a grand living space, with a large spacious kitchen that flowed into an expansive sitting room.

"Wow," Stanley said.

"Ohhhh!" Laura replied. She ambled through the kitchen, admiring the new appliances and huge island. Stanley put down the suitcase and followed.

"Look at this oven!" Laura said. "These things cost thousands of dollars."

"You lying," Stanley replied.

"No, I'm not," Laura said. "These are the ovens they put in houses on the home improvement channel."

She looked at the backsplash.

"They even have a pot filler!"

"Why can't you fill the pot at the sink?" Stanley asked.

"It's called convenience," Laura replied.

They walked into the great room. Laura ran her hands over every piece of furniture, while Stanley sat on the lounge sofa before the massive screen TV.

"Now this is what I'm talking about!" he said. "Where's the remote?"

"Come on, man," Laura said. "There's more to see."

She trotted down the hallway, inspecting each space.

"Each room has its own bathroom!" Laura said.

"If the regular rooms look like this, I can't imagine what the main suite looks like," Stanley replied.

"Let's find out!" Laura said.

They hurried through the great room, then climbed the stairs to the second floor. The master bedroom occupied the entire floor. It contained a king-sized bed, a huge ensuite, a sitting area, a mini kitchen, and a spacious balcony with outside chairs and a gas grill.

"This is way too much room," Stanley said.

"I know," Laura said. "It's perfect. We can stay up here the entire time. Except for that perfect kitchen."

"And that giant TV," Stanley added.

They went out on the balcony. The Atlantic Ocean lapped on the sparsely occupied beach, the temperature mild. A wide wooden boardwalk extended from the lower floor patio, crossing a patch of marsh, and ending at the small sand dunes peppered with swaying sea oats. Laura closed her eyes, listening to the waves.

"I'll get the rest of our stuff," Stanley said. "I know how you are when you get near the ocean."

"Okay," Laura said, her eyes still closed. She had no idea how much time passed between Stanley leaving her alone then calling out her name.

"What, Baby?"

"Come down to the kitchen," he said. "There's something you need to see."

Laura lingered on the balcony for a moment before going downstairs to the kitchen. They had been so focused on the appliances and other kitchen details that they missed the basket of wine and cookies sitting on the large island.

"Now this is sweet!" Laura grabbed a wine bottle from the basket, read the label, and whistled.

"This is good wine."

Stanley took a cookie from the basket. "Is this chocolate chip or raisin?"

Laura took a look. "Chocolate chip, I think."

Stanley shrugged then and ate it. "You were right. Good cookies, too."

Laura frowned at him. "Why are you eating a cookie? We're getting dinner in a few minutes."

"I'm a grown man," Stanley said. "If I want to eat a cookie, I'll eat a cookie."

Laura rolled her eyes as she punched her phone.

"Who are you calling?" Stanley asked.

"Janine," she said. "I need to let her know we're here."

"Good," Stanley replied. "I hope we can get her to make us some of her red rice and gumbo."

He ate another cookie and Laura glared at him. The phone buzzed and Janine answered.

"Laura? I didn't expect to hear from you this time of year."

"Me and Stanley decided to do something different. We're here."

"On Sea Island?"

"Yep, and we can't wait to come over to Gullah Kitchen and get us some red rice and gumbo."

"I'm afraid you won't be able to. I close the restaurant during the winter. Not enough visitors."

"That's terrible!"

"I know, but it is what it is. I'd end up spending more on the light bill than I would make selling food. Hey, how long y'all going to be here?"

"Until the day after Christmas."

"Where you staying?"

"A beach house in Palmetto Marsh."

"Ooh, chile! Did you win the lottery?"

Laura laughed. "Naw girl, we just decided to splurge."

"I tell you what, I'm busy with catering orders right now, but I'll bring you something before Christmas. How about that?"

"That sounds great! I don't want you going out of your way now."

"Ain't no problem," Janine said. "It won't take long, and I always wanted to see the insides of one of those big ol' houses."

"Let's do it!"

"I'll call you when I get started," Janine said.

"Great! Talk to you soon," Laura said.

"Bye, Laura!"

"Bye, Janine!"

Laura hung up with a big grin on her face.

"That's done! Now let's get something to eat before we settle in."

They went back to the SUV then headed out. Laura's phone buzzed and she checked.

"It's Bryce!"

She put the phone on speaker.

"Hey, Bryce!"

Instead of her son's voice, there was a giggle. "Hi, Grandma!"

"Cameron? Does your daddy know you're calling us?"

"No. He's asleep."

Laura looked serious. "Lord have mercy. What's wrong?"

"Daddy's sad," Cameron said. "I am, too."

"Why?"

"He misses Mommy," Cameron replied. "He doesn't say it, but I know it."

Laura looked at Stanley, and he shook his head.

"Well, Daddy will feel better soon," Laura said. "Don't you worry."

"Are you coming for Christmas?" Cameron asked.

"No, Grandma and Granddaddy are in Sea Island. We miss you, though."

"We miss you, too!" Cameron replied. "I wish I could come to Sea Island."

Laura's eyes went wide.

"Baby, let Grandma call you back."

"Okay Grandma. Bye!"

"Bye Cameron. I love you. Kisses!"

"Kisses!"

Laura hung up the phone.

"Bryce must be feeling really bad if the children noticed," she said.

"I know what you're thinking," Stanley replied. "We could afford it, but you know how proud he is."

"Well then, we don't ask him. We tell him."

Stanley pulled into the parking lot of one of their favorite Sea Island restaurants, Bone Creek Seafood Company. He took out his phone and called Bryce.

"Hey, Pop!" Bryce said, his voice groggy.

"Hey, Son! How you doing?"

"I'm good, Got the kids for the holidays. How you and Mama doing?"

"We're great. We decided to spend Christmas on Sea Island."

"That's a great idea! Is this the second honeymoon?"

Stanley laughed. "You can say that. Hey, me and your mama talked about it and we want you and the kids to come down and join us."

"Pop. You know my situation. I can't afford to. I need to be frugal until I find a new job."

"Your mama and I will get it. We have plenty of room, and you could use a break. You know how much you love it here."

"Pop, I can't ask you to do this."

"You're not asking. I'm telling. I'll send you the money in a few minutes."

"Pop, I . . ."

"Cameron called us," Laura said.

"What?!?"

"Don't get mad at him. He said you were sad. Now when your children know something's wrong, it's really wrong. So, you get those tickets, and you come on down, okay?"

"Okay. Thank y'all so much. I'll pay you back. I promise."

"Just come on down. We'll work out the details later. Bye, Son. Love you."

"Love y'all, too."

Stanley hung up and Laura smiled.

"Well, our big ol house won't be so empty," Laura said.

"And what's Christmas without kids?" Stanley replied.

"I know that's right!"

"This does mean I can't chase you around the house," Stanley said.

"Ha!" Laura replied. "Like I'd actually be running." She kissed his cheek. "We got plenty of time for that when we get back home. Right now, our baby boy needs us."

Stanley exited the car then hurried around to open Laura's door.

"Now let's get inside. I heard shrimp and grits calling me all the way in Atlanta."

"You so crazy," Laura said.

"And hungry, too."

Laura took Stanley's hand, and they strolled to join the long line of local folks waiting to enter Bone Creek.

-6-

Shelly was putting on her uniform when her phone buzzed. She saw Charlotte's name and her face scrunched up. She considered not answering, but curiosity won out.

"Hey," she said.

"Oh, so it's like that?" Charlotte replied. "You sound like your puppy died."

"Naw, I sound like a woman whose roommate deserted her and practically moved out."

"A girl gotta do what a girl gotta do," Charlotte replied.

"I can't believe you just went and moved in with him," Shelly said. "You don't know Javan like that."

"I do now," Charlotte replied.

Shelly couldn't help but laugh.

"Girl, you are wild."

"You were there. I couldn't let him leave without spending my time with him."

"I don't see how you did this," Shelly said. "You might not ever see him again."

"I might not," Charlotte agreed. "But I'm seeing him now. But let's talk about you. What happened between you and Damian after we left?"

"Nothing," Shelly said. "We agreed to stop seeing each other."

"No, uh uh," Charlotte replied. "No y'all didn't. Well, I know he didn't. That man is crazy about you."

"You're right, it was me," Shelly confessed. "I like him. I like him too much. I'm not ready for that kind of relationship."

"And will when you be ready?" Charlotte asked.

"Look, I gotta go to work," Shelly said. "And you should be doing the same thing."

"I requested a few days off and my commander approved it. I'll work through Christmas."

"Wow. You're really serious about this."

"Yes, I am," Charlotte said. "Javan Carter is going to miss me."

"I'm happy for y'all."

"Shelly don't let this pass," Charlotte said. "Sam is gone, sis. He's moved on, and you're standing still. You have a good brother waiting for you. Don't let him slip away."

"Bye, girl," Shelly said.

"Bye."

Shelly thought on Charlotte's words as she drove to the base. Damian was a good man, at least from what she'd seen. The only way she could know more would be to spend more time with him. Even if she did let him get close, she wouldn't go as far as Charlotte. Her chest tightened as she remembered Sam. She'd given their relationship one hundred percent and it still wasn't enough. That was her way; it was all or nothing. Was she ready to give her all again?

She reached the base with no answer to that question, but there was one thing that she did decide. She would ask for leave back to the States. She wanted to go home. She needed some time with folks whose love was unconditional. It was a long shot, but she was going to try. She wasn't spending another Christmas in Germany if she could help it.

Shelly saluted the NCOs absently as she made her way to her office. Closing the door behind her, she sat down then logged into her computer. The first thing she did was pull up the leave application and fill it out, listing a family emergency for the reason. And it was a family crisis in a sense. She needed to be with her family, or she was going to fall apart.

She emailed the document to HR then got about the day's business. The morning passed quickly; she took lunch in the mess hall, where they served their version of holiday food that wasn't half bad, except for the mac and cheese. As long as she lived, she would never get used to the runny concoction the Army mess hall served.

She returned to her office, writing reports and orders for her unit. There was a knock on her door, and she looked up to see her commanding officer, Lieutenant Colonel Logan Pierce. Shelly jumped to her feet then saluted.

"Sir, how can I help you?"

"At ease, Captain," he said. "I came to talk to you about this."

The CO held the printout of her leave request. Shelly's throat went dry.

"Ah yes, sir. My request. Is there a problem?"

"It's rather late," Pierce said. "Most holiday requests are submitted in September."

"I understand, sir," she said.

"So why the late submission?"

Shelly tried to think of a good reason, but she couldn't.

"I need to go home," she finally said. "I want to see my parents. I want to be with my family this year."

Colonel Pierce smiled. "That's the most honest answer I've heard in a long time. I know it's tough to be stationed abroad, especially this time of year. You're an excellent officer, and your unit is one of my best."

The colonel walked to her desk then held out his hand. Shelly was confused.

"A pen," Pierce said. "You do have one, don't you?"

"Of course, sir!"

Shelly opened her desk drawer, took out a pen then handed it to the colonel. He smiled as he signed the leave papers then handed them back to her.

"Have a good time," he said. "Tell your parents they did an outstanding job raising you. Merry Christmas."

"Thank you, sir!" Shelly said. "Merry Christmas to you, too."

The two exchanged salutes, Shelly struggling to control herself until the colonel was gone.

"Yes!"

She jumped up then did a few dance steps before settling into her chair and texting Charlotte.

Girl, I got holiday leave!
Excellent!

She dialed Mama, bouncing in her chair as she waited for her to answer.

"Hey, Baby!"

"Hey, Mama! Guess what? I'll be home for Christmas!"

"That's wonderful! Stanley! Shelly's coming home for Christmas!"

"Great!"

"That makes four," Mama said. "Bryce and the grandkids are coming too!"

"That's wonderful," Shelly said. She thought about how fun it would be to see Bryce and his children. She was glad April wouldn't be there. She never liked her. If only Terry would come home, too. That would make for a perfect Christmas.

"Looks like we got some cooking to do, Baby Girl."

"We sure do! Don't start without me."

"I won't."

"I gotta go, Mama," she said. "I'm still at work.

"Okay, Baby. Love you!"

"Love you too, Mama. Bye!"

The rest of the day flew by as she thought about all the things she needed to do before leaving. She called Bryce to let him know she was coming home; it was he who informed her that Mama and Daddy were at Sea Island. She was hoping to be in familiar surroundings, but then again Sea Island was their home away from home, so it would be okay. Next, she called Terry. She seemed interested but wouldn't say whether she would be home or not, so Shelly let it go. She wasn't going to let Terry's behavior kill her mood. There was no need to tell her they would be meeting at Sea Island; she probably wasn't coming anyway. As she hung up, she began clicking Damian's number then stopped. Why was she calling him? They agreed to stop seeing each other and he was spending his holidays country hopping. But then the words Charlotte said to her earlier began sinking in. Sam was the past; she was wasting her present brooding over him. But was Damian the one? She shook her head. It shouldn't be about him being the one. She was getting too far ahead of herself. She called him.

"Shelly? What's up?"

"Nothing. How are you?"

"I'm good. I didn't expect to hear from you."

"I know. Is it okay?"

"Of course. What's up?"

"I put in for leave and my commander signed off on it."

"That's good. So, you're going to the States?"

"Yes. I really miss my family."

"It's good you get to go. I hope you have fun."

"I will."

They were quiet for a moment.

"Why don't you come with me?"

"What?"

"Come home with me. My parents rented a house on Sea Island. They have plenty of room and I'm sure they won't mind."

"Wait a minute. A few days ago, we said we should stop seeing each other. And now you want me to come home with you?"

"I know it sounds a little crazy, but that's the kind of person I am. It's all or nothing. So, what do you want to do?"

"Well . . . okay. As long as it's cool with your parents."

"It will be. I'll set everything up. This is going to fun."

"So, I guess we're seeing each other again?"

Shelly laughed. "Yeah, I think so."

"Cool. See you tonight."

"Okay."

Shelly hung up then stared at her phone. A twinge of nervousness hit her in the gut.

"Girl, I hope you know what you're doing."

A Palmetto Christmas

-7-

Stanley checked his watch as he waited for Bryce and the kids at Savannah/Hilton Head Airport baggage claim. Their flight had been delayed in Atlanta, but only for an hour. He passed the time by taking a quick tour of the modest airport and buying a bag of pecans. He was munching on them when he heard a squeal.

"Grandpa!"

He looked up to see the grandkids running toward him, their backpacks bouncing off their backs. Bryce strolled behind them, a wide smile on his bearded face. Stanley squatted and opened his arms, catching the little ones in his embrace.

"Hey, hey, hey!" he said. He stood, lifting both kids off the ground.

"Alright now, Old Man," Bryce said. "Don't hurt yourself."

"I already have," Stanley replied.

"Come on, y'all," Bryce said. He took the children then lowered them to the terrazzo. Stanley and Bryce hugged.

"Missed you, Boy," Stanley said.

"Missed you too, Pop."

Stanley drew back his head then rubbed his own chin.

"What's all this? You look older than me."

Bryce chuckled. "It's the style. You should grow one."

Stanley laughed. "Your mama hates beards. She'd be at me with a razor the first sign of a whisker."

"It's your face," Bryce said.

"No, it's not," Stanley replied. "I gave it away forty years ago."

He grasped the children's hands.

"Come on. Let's get y'all's bags."

They walked to the carousel and picked up the bags. Stanley led them to the parking lot.

"New ride?" Bryce asked.

"Naw. We rented it for the trip. Good thing we did. Our little car couldn't hold all y'all."

They loaded the luggage then strapped the children into their seats.

"I'll drive," Bryce said.

"Naw, I got it," Stanley replied. "You know how I am about that."

"I'm the same way," Bryce said.

"At least you got it honest. Now get in that passenger seat."

In minutes they were on their way to Sea Island.

"So, when is Shelly arriving?" Bryce asked.

"This afternoon," Stanley replied. "She's bringing a friend. A boyfriend."

Bryce's eyebrows rose. "Is she now?"

Stanley nodded. "I don't know how I feel about that. She told your mama first and she said it was fine."

"She's a grown woman, Pop."

"I know, but they ain't sleeping together. Not in my house. We got plenty of room."

Bryce laughed. "Did y'all hear anything from Terry?"

Stanley frowned. "No. But I've stopped waiting. That girl does what she wants to do. She always has. And apparently, she doesn't want to come home anymore."

A Palmetto Christmas

The two were quiet for the rest of the drive, the children playing and chatting along the way. Bryce looked at the passing sights and grinned. This was a good idea. His problems would be waiting for him when he returned to Chicago, but at that moment they were as far away as the moon.

They entered Palmetto Marsh, Stanley weaving through the narrow roads until they reached the beach house.

"Wow!" Bryce said. "This is huge!"

"Wait until you see inside," Stanley replied.

"We want to go to the beach!" the children yelled.

"We will," Bryce replied. "But first we have to see your grandma and get settled."

Stanley and Bryce were unloading the SUV when the front door opened, and Laura stepped outside.

"There they are!" Laura wore a light pink sweatshirt with khaki pants that stopped at her calves. Her house shoes matched her sweatshirt.

The children ran to her then hugged her legs. Bryce trotted up, adding his hug.

"Mama," he whispered.

"Brycie," she replied.

Stanley walked by with the luggage.

"I could use some help," he said.

"Let's get y'all inside," Laura said. "I have fresh baked cookies!"

Bryce went to the SUV and unloaded the rest of the luggage. Stanley led him to the children's room, then took him to his.

"Good to have you here," he said to Bryce. "Wish there was one more."

"C'mon, Pop," Bryce said. "That's done. I know how much y'all loved April. I did, too. But it's over."

"I'm sorry," Stanley said. "How you handling things?"

"Not as good as I hoped," Bryce said.

He sat on the bed and Stanley took the chair beside it.

"I always thought if I worked hard, I would never be in a situation like this. And the worst thing is that it had nothing to do with my skills. We get bought out and I'm out of a job, just like that."

"It's not about the job," Stanley said. "They can't take what's the most important. That's up here." Stanley tapped his head. "There's somebody else out there that's willing to pay more than your old job. You just need to find them."

"I wish it was that simple," Bryce replied. "There are a few places I can think of, but none of them are in Chicago. I don't want to be too far away from the kids."

Stanley stood then patted Bryce's shoulder.

"Things will work themselves out. Just keep looking and keep praying. And don't hesitate to ask us for help."

"I don't want to be a burden," Bryce said.

"You're not, you're our son. Plus, we ain't broke. Look at this big ass house we rented."

Bryce laughed as he stood.

"Thank you, Pop."

"Don't mention it. Now let's get in that kitchen and get some cookies before your greedy kids eat them all."

Laura and the kids sat at the island, eating cookies and drinking milk. Bryce and Stanley reached for the dishes.

"Un uh!" Laura said. "Use the paper plates. I'm not washing dishes the whole vacation."

They got their cookies then sat at the dinette.

"So, Shelly will be in this afternoon?" Bryce asked.

"Yes," Laura replied. "You think you can pick her up at the airport?"

"No problem," Bryce said. "That way I get to check out this man she's bringing."

"I'm sure he'll be fine," Laura said. "I trust Shelly. Now let's finish these cookies so we can take a walk on the beach."

"Isn't it a bit chilly?" Bryce asked.

Laura's eyes narrowed. "I can't believe a man who lives in Chicago would be scared of a little chill."

"Not me. I'm looking out for y'all."

Laura finished her cookie. "I'll go get our jackets just in case."

They donned their jackets then went out the back door, walking across the boardwalk bordered by dunes and grass to the beach.

* * *

Shelly glanced at Damian as their plane circled the airport. He'd slept the entire journey, only waking up when they changed flights in Atlanta. Even then he was mostly quiet. Her nervousness made her stomach roiled. This was a bad idea. She wasn't Charlotte. She should have just come home and let Damian do whatever he was going to do. He probably didn't even want to come. He was just being nice.

She shook her doubts away. Of course, he wanted to be with her. Who would spend that much money on something they didn't want to do? Plus, she knew he liked her. And he was going to meet her family. This was good, she thought. Very good.

The pilot's announcement of their final approach woke him. He stretched, yawned, opened his eyes, turned his head, and smiled.

"Hi. We there yet?"

Damian's grin wiped away her doubts.

"We're landing," she said.

"Good. I'm tired of flying."

Shelly laughed. "How can you be tired? You slept the entire time!"

"See? That's how tired I was."

The plane landed a few minutes later. Shelly texted daddy and he texted back letting her know Bryce was picking them up. She grabbed Damian's arm.

"Come on! My brother is picking us up!"

Bryce was waiting at baggage claim, his bright smile like a salve.

"Hey, Sis!" he said.

They hugged, rocking from side to side like they always did.

"It's so good see you!" she said.

"It's good to see you, too."

Bryce held her for a few more seconds then let her go. Damian stood a few feet away, looking like a scared puppy. Bryce could be intimidating; at six foot four and still mostly muscle he made an impression. Shelly lowered her head to hide her grin as Bryce's demeanor transformed from playful to serious. He extended his hand.

"I'm Bryce, Shelly's brother."

"Damian Cole."

Bryce grasped Damian's hand then pulled him into a hug.

"What's up, bruh?" he said.

Shelly watched the tension ease from Damian's face.

"It's all good."

Bryce let Damian go.

"I ain't gonna give you the third degree," he said. "That's Pop's job. I trust my baby sister's judgement. Now let's get out of here."

Shelly and Damian followed Bryce to the SUV. Shelly climbed into the passenger side while Damian helped Bryce with the luggage. Damian slid into the back and Bryce jumped into the driver's seat.

"So which way?" he asked. "Highway or scenic route?"

Shelly turned around to look at Damian.

"You ever been to the Low Country?"

"No."

She turned to Bryce. "Scenic route it is!"

They left the airport and were soon travelling the same back roads their parents took to the island.

"So, Damian, how did you meet my sister?" Bryce asked.

"Through a friend," Damian replied. "He's dating Charlotte."

"Charlotte is my bestie," Shelly said.

Bryce nodded. "You Army, too?"

"No, Air Force," Damian replied.

"So, they allow inter-service relationships?"

Damian and Shelly laughed.

"Our bases are nearby," Shelly said. "As long as one of us doesn't outrank the other, it's all good."

"What about you, Bryce? Did you serve?" Damian asked.

"Hold up now, brother, you're the boyfriend and I'm the brother. I ask the questions."

Shelly punched Bryce's shoulder and he laughed.

"Seriously though, I never considered the military. Earned a football scholarship to Grambling, but just missed going pro. Ended up in tech instead."

"You look like it," Damian commented.

"Jock or nerd?" Bryce asked. "Be careful how you answer."

"Quit messing with him!" Shelly scolded. She turned and gave Damian a smile. "Excuse my brother. He's a fool."

Bryce chuckled. "Y'all enjoy the scenery. We're at the good part now."

They cruised through the marshlands. Shelly rolled down the window, taking in the pungent fragrance. She closed her eyes for a moment and felt the tension of the past few months fading.

"This is beautiful," Damian said.

"Where are you from, bruh?" Bryce asked.

"Tulsa," Damian replied.

"That's a long way from the ocean."

"Tell me about it. That's one reason I joined the Air Force. I wanted to travel on Uncle Sam's dime. Plus, I've been saving up to go to college once I get out."

"So, you don't plan on doing the twenty?"

"No sir. Majoring in business. I want to be an entrepreneur."

"You're just saying that to get on my good side."

"You're always talking about people owning their own business, yet here you are still working for 'The Man,'" Shelly said.

"I just haven't found the right time to do it," Bryce replied. "Too many things going on."

"There's never a right time. Isn't that what you used to tell me?" Shelly said.

Bryce looked into the rear-view mirror at Damian. "She never forgets anything. It's annoying as hell. Remember that."

"Be quiet, boy!"

Shelly's attention drifted back to the road, enjoying the live oaks with their Spanish moss peppered canopies, palmetto shrubs and grasses filling the gaps between them. The road curved to the right, revealing a small wooden building with a faded sign on the roof.

"Bryce! Stop here!"

"What? Where?"

Shelly pointed at the building. "Right there!"

Bryce checked behind him before slowing quickly and swinging into the gravel parking lot.

"Come on, y'all!" Shelly said.

She jumped out of the car and hurried inside the building. Bryce and Damian followed.

"What's going on?" Damian asked.

"I have no idea," Bryce replied.

They caught up with Shelly. It was a small convenience store, its shelves stacked with various foods and snacks. Shelly stood by the checkout counter with a big grin on her face. An older woman behind the counter faced her. Behind her was a young man that resembled her, probably her son. Both shared the deep brown skin common among the Gullah folks in the region. Both shared friendly smiles.

"Don't tell me you don't remember this store?" Shelly said to Bryce.

Bryce shrugged. "Actually, I don't."

Shelly planted her hands on her waist. "Come on, Bryce! This used to be the only store between Savannah and Sea Island."

The woman nodded her head and Shelly gestured at her.

"See?"

Damian perused the shelves. "I don't see anything special."

"That's because you're looking in the wrong place," Shelly replied. She picked up a covered dish that sat on the counter. On the plate were two dozen small brown square pastries.

"These are delicious! Mama used to make Daddy stop so we could get a plate to take to the condo."

The woman walked from behind the counter.

"Y'all lucky," she said. "We don't have these all the time. I can make them, but my mama makes them right."

Shelly extended her hand. The woman pushed her hand aside and gave her a hug.

"I'm Martha," she said.

"I'm Shelly. How much will that plate cost me?"

The woman drew back, a surprised look on her face.

"You want all of them?"

Shelly nodded. "Every last one. Our family's gathering for Christmas on Sea Island. It's a bunch of us."

"I can sell you the whole plate for thirty dollars."

Bryce's eyes bucked. "Thirty dollars?!? That's . . ."

"Just about right," Shelly finished. "And I'd like to place an order for another plate if possible."

Shelly winked at Bryce. "Unlike you, I still have a job."

"That's cold," Bryce replied.

"Terrence, pack these up for this nice young lady." Martha said to the young man.

"Yes, ma'am," he replied.

Terrence took the plate off the counter. Shelly was reaching into her purse when Damian stepped forward.

"I got this," he said. He handed Miss Martha his card. Shelly smiled.

"Terrence, can I get three of those . . . what do you call them?"

"Chewies," Miss Martha said.

Terrence took three of the squares, placed them on a napkin and gave them to Shelly. She gave Bryce one and he stuffed the whole square in his mouth. His eyes lit up as he chewed.

"This is good!"

She took another and extended it toward Damian's mouth.

"Want a taste?"

"Of course." Damian bit half the square. "This is good. It's sweet, like you."

"Okay. Calm down you two," Bryce interrupted. "Let's get back on the road."

Terrence gave Shelly the chewies.

"When should I come back?" she asked Miss Martha.

"In three days," the woman replied. "Here's my number."

Miss Martha pulled up her ecard on her phone and Shelly scanned it.

"See y'all then!" she said.

They returned to the SUV and continued to the house. Shelly's tension eased further as they drove across the bridge spanning the mainland and Sea Island.

"This is beautiful," Damian said. "I see why you love it."

"You haven't seen the best part," Shelly said. "This is our home away from home."

"It is," Bryce said. "I have to say I'm glad Mama and Daddy talked us into coming."

He glanced at Shelly. "You talk to Terry lately?"

"I talked to her last week," Shelly replied.

"Who's Terry?" Damian asked.

"Our big sister," Bryce replied. "She's an artist. A pretty good one, too."

"She doesn't come home that often," Shelly said. "She travels a lot."

"And she doesn't get along with our parents that well," Bryce said.

"I know that feeling," Damian commented.

Bryce was about to open his mouth but Shelly touched his shoulder then shook her head. That was a subject she and Damian hadn't discussed, and she didn't want to, at least not yet. Maybe after they got to know each other better.

The familiar sights continued as they drove down the four-lane that divided the island into equal halves. Bryce slowed down and entered the turning lane for Palmetto Marsh.

"Wait," Shelly said. "Mama and Daddy rented a place here?"

Bryce smirked. "Wait until you see the house."

They followed the winding road through the well-manicured grounds, the golf cart paths running parallel to the road busy with carts, walkers, and runners. Bryce slowed as they approached the guard gate. The guard peered inside, saw their pass, then waved them on. Bryce took a left turn, driving down a narrow street with large homes facing the beach.

"Oh, my goodness!" Shelly said.

Bryce pulled into the driveway of one of the largest homes.

"Here we are!" Bryce announced.

They climbed out of the SUV, Shelly taking a moment to savor the beauty of the home and the immaculate landscaping. Damian walked up beside her.

"You didn't tell me your parents are rich," he said.

"They're not," Shelly said. She turned to Bryce, who was taking their luggage out of the SUV.

"Bryce, what is this?"

"You'll have to ask them," he replied. "I'm just rolling with it."

"There goes our inheritance," Shelly joked.

"All five dollars of it," Bryce replied.

Bryce honked the car horn. Moments later the door opened and the family spilled out. Bryce's children ran to him with hugs and kisses as if he'd been gone for days. Mama and Daddy were close behind, bright smiles on their faces. They both went straight to Shelly.

"Baby Girl!" Stanley said.

He wrapped her in a big hug and Shelly pressed her head against his chest.

"Hey Daddy! It's so good to be home!"

Laura stepped in when Daddy stepped away.

"Hey little lady! I missed you!"

"I missed you too, Mama."

Laura and Stanley turned their attention to Damian.

"Mama, Daddy, this is Damian Cole."

Damian extended his hand. "Please to mee you."

Laura slapped Damian's hand aside and hugged him.

"We don't play that here," she said. "Welcome."

Daddy approached Damian with his hand extended. Damian grabbed his hand and they shook.

"Welcome," Stanley said. "We'll talk later."

Shelly frowned. "Daddy don't be like that. Damian's cool."

"We'll see," Stanley replied.

"It's okay," Damian said. "I know the drill."

Stanley half smiled and nodded. "We'll get y'all luggage. Y'all ladies go on inside."

"Wait," Shelly said. She went to the SUV and got the treats.

"Look what I got!" she said.

"Chewies? Where did you find them?" Laura asked.

"At the old store we used to stop all the time."

"Did y'all come the back way?" Laura asked.

"Yes, ma'am," Shelly answered.

"I must not have been paying attention," Laura replied.

"You were probably asleep," Stanley said as he walked by with luggage.

Laura frowned. "I never fall asleep when we're traveling."

"How do you know?" Stanley said. "You're asleep. I'm trying to listen to Al Green over your snoring."

Laura and Shelly laughed. Shelly pulled back the wrapping.

"Get one."

Laura shook her head. "No chile. We're gonna save those for Christmas Eve."

Shelly smiled mischievously. "I ordered another plate. We pick it up in two days."

"Well in that case . . ."

Laura grabbed a chewie from the plate and stuffed it in her mouth.

"They're just as good! Babies, y'all come taste this!"

The children scurried over to Shelly and Laura, and Laura gave them a chewie. Bryce, Damian, and

Stanley took the luggage inside, followed by the ladies and the children.

Shelly's mouth dropped open. "This is beautiful!" she said.

"Ain't it though?" Laura replied. "Come look at this kitchen!"

Laura gave Shelly and Damian a tour of the kitchen and the rest of downstairs while Stanley waited in the foyer for them to return.

"Shelly, your room is down there," Stanley said. "Damian, your room is over here."

Their rooms were on opposite sides of the house. Shelly and Damian held back a laugh.

"Okay, Daddy," Shelly said.

"Thank you for allowing me to stay IN the house," Damian said.

Stanley smirked then laughed. "Oh, so you got jokes."

Shelly and Damian carried their luggage to their rooms. Bryce took the kids outside to the beach. Laura and Stanley watched them go.

"You know, this was supposed to be our special vacation," Stanley said.

"I know," Laura replied. "But I'm glad everyone's here. That's what the holidays are all about."

"Almost everyone," Stanley said.

The silence after his statement was heavy.

"Maybe she'll come this year," Laura said.

"Don't get your hopes up," Stanley replied.

Shelly and Damian returned to the foyer about the same time.

"Damian, do you like football?" Stanley asked.

"Yes, sir," Damian replied.

Stanley smiled. "I like you better already. C'mon. Let's break in this big ass TV."

Shelly waved at Damian as he walked away with Daddy.

"Now you come in this kitchen so we can plan what we're cooking for everybody."

"You putting me right to work?" Shelly asked. "Right after I brought you chewies?"

Laura laughed. "I'm sorry, baby. You're probably tired from all that flying. Go on and lay down. This ain't going nowhere."

Shelly was returning to her room when Laura touched her shoulder.

"You talked to Terry lately?"

"Last week," Shelly said.

"How's she doing?"

"You should call and ask her," Shelly said. "She's got the same number."

Laura waved her hand. "Terry don't want to talk to me or your daddy."

"You should call her and find out," Shelly said.

Laura didn't reply. Instead, she turned toward the kitchen and walked away.

"I asked her to come home for Christmas," Shelly said.

Laura turned around, a hopeful look on her face. "What did she say?"

"She said she'd think about it."

Laura's smile faded.

"That means she's not coming."

"You don't know that, Mama."

"I know Terry. She doesn't have to 'think' about anything. Either she does it or she doesn't do it."

Laura returned to the kitchen.

"You go on get some rest, Shelly."

"Yes, Mama."

Shelly watched Mama until she disappeared into the kitchen, before going to her room. Mama was right; Terry wasn't one to be undecisive. But hopefully this time, Mama was wrong.

-8-

Terry and João sat in the rental car in her parents' driveway, Terry staring at the front door. It had been ten years since she walked out those doors, vowing never to return. Now here she was back again, reliving bitter memories.

"So, are we going to the door?" João asked.

"Yes. In a minute," she replied.

"We've been sitting here for thirty minutes," he said. "The neighbors are probably suspicious."

"Let them be," Terry said.

"They might call the police," João replied. "I would."

"I wonder if they're home?" Terry said.

"Who? The neighbors?" João asked.

"No, my parents. We've been sitting in here forever and no one has come outside."

"Maybe they called the police," João said.

"Stop it with the police already," Terry replied. Terry closed her eyes then braced herself.

"Let's do this," she said.

She opened the car door and stepped outside. There was a slight chill in the air and she shivered. She wasn't sure if it was the weather or her apprehension. She walked up the driveway to the door.

"Terry?"

She looked to the left to see Mrs. Wingate standing on her front porch with a wide smile on her face.

"My goodness! I haven't seen you in years!"

"Hello, Mrs. Wingate," Terry said, trying to cover the annoyance in her voice.

Mrs. Wingate opened her front door.
"Bill! Come out here! It's Terry!"
"Who?"
"Terry! Laura and Stan's daughter!"
"Oh, that Terry!"
Mr. Wingate appeared moments later and the couple made their way over. This was not what Terry planned, but she put on her best happy-to-see-you face. Her hesitancy disappeared when she hugged them. It felt good to hold people that really knew her.

She heard the car door close and turned to see João coming around the car with his ever-present smile.

"Can I get some love, too?" he said.

The Wingates looked skeptical.

"This is my boyfriend, João."

Mr. Wingate extended his hand and João pulled him into a hug. Mr. Wingate smiled despite himself. João then smothered Mrs. Wingate with a hug. They both laughed afterwards.

"You're quite friendly," Mrs. Wingate said.

"I'm just so happy to meet someone who knows my Terry," João replied. "She's met my family, but I've never met hers."

"We're not exactly family," Mr. Wingate said.

"You are neighbors!" João replied. "Where I'm from it's the same thing."

"Where are you from?" Mr. Wingate asked.

"São Paulo, Brazil."

Mrs. Wingate's eyes got big. "Wait a minute. I knew I recognized you. You're João Santo Rebeiro! The Traveling Chef on the Food Channel!"

João beamed. "Guilty as charged."

Terry usually let João bask in the attention of his fans, but she wanted to get things over with.

"If y'all will excuse us," she said.

"Your parents aren't at home," Mrs. Wingate said.

"Oh, did they go out?" Terry asked.

"We think they're out of town," Mr. Wingate said. "We haven't seen them for a few days. They usually let us know so we can keep an eye on things, but this time they didn't."

"You have their number, don't you?" Terry asked.

"Why didn't you think of that, Bill?" Mrs. Wingate asked.

"I usually don't have to."

"I'll call them," Terry said. "Excuse me." She walked away as she took her phone from her purse. Terry had no intention of calling her parents, and she didn't want the Wingates to call them, either. That would mean she would have to speak to them and she wasn't sure she was ready, even though she stood in their driveway. She called Shelly instead.

"Hey girl!" Shelly said. "What you up to?"

"I'm home," Terry replied.

"What?!?"

"I'm home. Standing in front of the house."

"In Atlanta?"

"Yes, and it looks like Mama and Daddy aren't here."

"They're not! All of us are at Sea Island!"

"What?!? Why didn't you tell me?"

"I didn't' think you would come. So, you coming down?"

"I've come this far. Text me the address."

"Okay!"

"And don't tell Mama and Daddy. I want it to be a surprise."

"You sure?"

"Yes. Love you, Sis."
"Love you, too!"

Terry hung up. "Mystery solved. Mama and Daddy decided to take a Christmas vacation to Sea Island. Bryce and Shelly are down there with them."

"That sounds great!" Mrs. Wingate said. "Looks like the whole family will be together for the holidays."

"We will," Terry replied. "I guess we better be getting on our way. It's a long trip."

"You know, we have a key to the house and the security code," Mr. Wingate said. "I don't think your parents would mind y'all spending the night. It's long drive to Sea Island."

"And y'all can come over for dinner," Mrs. Wingate added.

Terry looked at João. "What do you think?"

"I think it's a wonderful idea!" he said.

"Looks like we're spending the night then," Terry said.

Mrs. Wingate went back inside her house and returned with the key and security code. Terry took them then went to the front porch, each step an eternity. She unlocked the front door then walked inside. The alarm was nearby; she shut it off and stepped back in time. Everything was the same as the day she left, except for a few small items.

"This is wonderful," João said. "Your parents have done well."

"They have."

"I grew up in the favelas, but you know this."

"You've come a long way," Terry said.

"We both have."

Terry walked upstairs to her old room. The bed comforter was different, but nothing else had changed. Her academic and athletic trophies and awards still decorated the walls, as did pictures of her with her high school and college basketball teams.

"You were beautiful then, and you're beautiful now," João said.

"Thank you," Terry replied.

He came up behind her, wrapping his arms around her waist.

"This is good, no?"

"It is," she replied. "I don't know how it's going to go when I see them."

"Everything will be fine," he said.

"I hope so," Terry replied. She turned her head and they kissed.

"Now let's get washed up. We have a dinner invitation. And be nice. I don't remember Mrs. Wingate being the best cook in the world."

"If she's been watching my show, I'm sure her skills have improved."

"You're so vain," Terry said.

"Is that what you call telling the truth?"

"Come on, boy."

Terry and João freshened up then walked over to the Wingates for dinner. It was a simple meal and surprisingly good; João had no complaints. After the meal they retired to the family room. Mrs. Wingate opened a bottle of wine as Mr. Wingate went to their old record player.

"What kind of music do you like?" he asked.

"I'm partial to jazz myself," Terry replied.

"You don't have to say that for our sake," Mr. Wingate replied.

"No really, I love jazz," Terry said. "The older the better."

"Now that's music to my ears," Mr. Wingate said with a smile. "How 'bout some Coltrane?"

"Perfect," Terry and João said in unison.

Mr. Wingate took the vinyl album from its cover and put it on the player. The smooth music helped Terry relax.

They sat around the small coffee table.

"So how are the kids?" Terry asked.

"They're good," Mrs. Wingate said. "Kadeem is living in Savannah. Lacey's here in Metro Atlanta, and Jon Jon lives in Miami."

A smirk came to Mrs. Wingate face. Terry knew what she was going to say before the words left her mouth.

"That boy was crazy about you."

"Yes, he was," Mr. Wingate seconded. "I was hoping you were gonna become part of the family."

"Hey, I'm sitting right here," João said.

"The entire neighborhood loved them some Terry," Mrs. Wingate said.

"I understand why," João replied. "She is a lovely woman, inside and out."

Terry laughed nervously. Talking about her looks made her uncomfortable. She had nothing to do with her appearance. It was as much a hindrance as it was a help. She had a difficult time getting people to see beyond her looks and notice her talent. João was the first man that approached her that didn't mention her appearance. It was her art that caught his eye. Maybe it was because he was a handsome man and was used to such things, or maybe it was because such things didn't rank high on his list. Whatever it was, it was refreshing. It was one of the reasons she loved him.

"So, what are you up to these days?" Mrs. Wingate asked.

"I'm an artist," Terry replied.

"Excellent!"

"She's being modest," João said. "Terry is one of the top abstract artists in North America, possibly the world. Her art hangs in some of the best international galleries. They sell for thousands of dollars."

Mr. Wingate clapped. "Congratulations! I always thought you should pursue your art. It's your passion. Stanley was always talking about you needed a real job, but I was like 'let that girl do what she wants.'"

"Thank you for that," Terry said. "He didn't exactly listen, but we got here anyway."

"Well, let's not talk about that," Mrs. Wingate said. She knew about the tension between Terry and her parents and her career choices. It was the reason she left . . . no, fled home and returned sparingly since.

"I don't want to have to reseal this wine, so let's drink it up and enjoy the company."

João raised his glass.

"Here here!"

They finished the wine, then Terry and João said their goodbyes. When they returned to the house, Terry went to the kitchen, searching inside the refrigerator until she found what she knew would be there; a plastic container filled with tuna fish salad. She took it out then proceeded to make a sandwich.

"Make me one, too," João said.

"It's just a tuna fish sandwich," Terry warned.

"I grew up in a favela, remember?" he said.

Terry made João a sandwich. They sat at the island and ate.

"This is good," João said, his mouth full.

"Enjoy it," Terry replied. "It's the closest I'll come to cooking anything."

João laughed.

"How is your visit home?" he asked.

"Good . . . so far," she replied. "It was nice sitting with the Wingates. Reminded me of the good things about growing up here."

"You grew up surrounded by people that love you," João said. "That is not as common as it should be."

"I know," Terry agreed. "But it still wasn't perfect."

"Things will work out," João said. "It all begins tomorrow. In the meantime, I sure would like another tuna fish sandwich."

Terry grinned. "Coming right up!"

As Terry made them another sandwich, she fought back the nervousness trying to creep into her mood. Things would be all right, she hoped. If not, she doubted if she would ever return home again.

-9-

Bryce woke up to a crowded bed. The children had once again abandoned their bunk beds and crawled into his space while he slept, taking advantage of the fact that he slept like a stone. He smiled as he looked at their peaceful faces, the only time they would be so for the rest of the day. They were the only good things that had come from his marriage. At least that's how he felt at the moment.

The smell of bacon and coffee stirred his senses and he sat up and stretched. Bryce got out of bed, careful not to wake up the children. He threw on his housecoat then ambled to the kitchen. Mama and Shelly chatted while they prepared breakfast. It reminded Bryce of when they were kids. Shelly would follow Mama around, imitating her as she prepared breakfast and their lunches. Damian sat at the island, his eyes on Shelly, a smile on his face.

"Morning," he said.

"Morning," everyone replied.

Bryce made himself a cup of coffee then sat with Damian.

"Still drinking coffee with your sugar?" Shelly asked.

"You know it," Bryce replied.

"Might as well drink hot Kool-Aid," she joked.

"When they make coffee flavor, I will. Where's Pop?"

"He's out walking on the beach," Laura said.

"Really? It's kinda chilly out there."

"You don't have to tell me," Laura replied. "I was out there with him like a fool."

Bryce finished his coffee then pushed away from the table.

"I'm going to join him."

"Good. Breakfast is almost ready. You can bring him back."

Bryce went back to his room for his sweats, tennis shoes and jacket. The children were still asleep. He was sure Mama would wake them for breakfast. He walked through the family room then out of the sliding doors, passed the pool that was too cold to use then across the private wooden walkway to the beach. The gentle waves lapped the wide expanse of sand, the wind blowing the spray toward him. Not knowing which way Pop went, he decided to jog to his left for a mile or so. If he didn't see Pop, he'd turn around and try the other direction.

Bryce was half a mile into his run when he saw him.

"Pop!"

Stanley turned around then waved him on. Bryce kept running until he reached him.

"Hey, Son!"

"Hey, Pop!"

They hugged then walked together.

"Mama said breakfast is almost ready.

Stanley nodded. "Let me get a few more steps in then we'll head back."

Bryce nodded.

"I'm glad you came out," Stanley said. "Gives us a chance to talk. How you doing?"

"I'm good," Bryce said.

"No, I mean how you feeling?"

Bryce shrugged. "As well as can be expected. The shutdown threw me for a loop."

"I can imagine," Stanley said. "I've been laid off before. They give you a severance?"

"Yeah," Bryce replied. "I'll be good for six months."

"Is it gonna take you that long to find something else?"

"No. To be honest, I could have a job tomorrow if I wanted it. But not in Chicago."

"Oh," Stanley said. "Trying to stay close to April and the kids."

Bryce nodded. "The kids, not April. The further away I am, the less I'll see them."

"I guess there's no chance of the two of you reconciling."

"No," Bryce said, trying to keep the bitterness from his voice. "She's moved on."

Stanley put his arm on Bryce's shoulder.

"You lose a woman two times. The first time when she leaves you. The second time when she finds someone else."

"Tell me about it," Bryc replied.

"Look, you know me and your Mama are here for you. Whatever you need, just let us know. And don't restrict your opportunities because of the situation. Moving ain't idea, but being unemployed is worse, for you and the kids. Y'all are in this situation together. Everybody will have to adjust. It won't be perfect, but you can make it work."

"I'm thinking about starting my own business, Pop," Bryce said. "I'm good at what I do, and I know quite a few of our clients aren't happy with our new owners."

Stanley whistled. "That's a big decision. You might want to think about it for a while."

"You don't think I can do it?"

"No. I know you can do it," Stanley said. "But having a business takes a lot of time and focus. It's going to be tough with the kids."

"You're right," Bryce said. "Just another option I'm considering."

Stanley's stomach growled and he laughed. "Looks like we're headed in the right direction."

The family was enjoying breakfast when they returned to the house. The kids waved their forks, and everyone else nodded with full mouths. Bryce and Stanley fixed their plates then sat at the island to eat.

"This is good as always, Mama," Bryce said.

"It sure is, Mrs. Jacobs," Damian agreed.

"Everything's better when I'm cooking with my baby," Laura said, cutting her eyes at Shelly.

"I could say the same thing about you," Shelly replied to Mama. "I can't ever get my grits as creamy as yours."

"That's because you trying to measure stuff out," Laura said. "You have to cook with your eyes and your heart."

"When I try that, I usually set the kitchen on fire," Bryce said. "I need instructions."

"It's called a recipe, brother," Shelly said.

"See?"

Laura pointed her fork at Bryce. "I need you to run by the store for me when you're done."

"Okay," Bryce replied reflexively.

"Mama! You still sending Bryce to the store?"

"He's still my son, ain't he?"

Bryce laughed. "It's fine. I'll take your grandchildren with me."

"No, you won't," Stanley said. "They want to stay and play on the beach with Grandpa, don't y'all?"

"Yeah!!!" the children answered.

Bryce went back for seconds. "I'll go when I finish. You can text me the list."

"Text you?" Laura said.

"I'll do it," Shelly said.

Bryce finished his plate then set out for the grocery store. It was good to be alone, even if only for a few minutes. When the kids went to spend time with April, he felt lonely. Here, it was peaceful.

He parked in front of the grocery store. His phone buzzed as he stepped out of the car and he checked his texts. Shelly had sent him a buggy sized list. Though the local grocery store chain was in Chicago, it was arranged differently. It took him a minute to find the vegetables.

He was inspecting the collards when a woman walked by him. He looked at her instinctively and his eyes flashed in recognition.

"No, it can't be," he whispered.

The woman had her back to him, so he waited until she moved to where he could see her. He smiled when his thoughts were confirmed.

"India!" he said.

The deep brown woman stared at him blankly for a second, then a smile slowly came to her face as her eyes softened.

"Bryce? Oh, my goodness. Bryce!"

Bryce strode to India and they hugged.

"What are you doing here?" India asked.

"Family vacation," he replied. "And you? Still living on the island?"

India shook her head. "Visiting, too. I'm home for Christmas. I live in Charlotte now."

They stepped back from each other, their eyes still locked. India was his vacation crush for his entire high school years. No matter when they came to the island, and no matter who he was dating at home, they always found each other. That week was theirs. The last time he saw her was the summer before his college freshman year. That was the week their relationship almost went to the next level.

"You look good," Bryce said.

"You too," India replied. "So where are you calling home these days? Still in the ATL?"

"No. After college I followed an internship to Chicago. Been there ever since."

"Chicago? Ugh." India hugged herself then shivered. "Too cold for an island girl."

"You get used to it," Bryce replied.

"Really?"

Bryce laughed. "No."

Bryce glanced at India's hands.

"No ring, I see."

India shared a sly grin. "No. Haven't found anyone worthy."

"So, you're single?"

"There's someone. It's recent. Still feeling each other out. How about you?"

"I was married but it didn't take. We divorced two years ago."

"I'm sorry."

Bryce shrugged. "It was for the best. We have two kids, a boy, and a girl."

"Let me see!"

Bryce tried to find a photo without April but couldn't. He shared a photo when they were still married.

"Oh, they're so cute!" India said. "And your ex is pretty."

"Yeah," he replied.

"Did they come with you?"

"Yeah. They're at the beach house being spoiled by their grandparents. So, are you staying with your parents?"

"Yes, it's been a while since I've spent the holidays at home."

"I guess you have plenty of vacation time."

"As much as I like," India said. "I own a tech consulting business. My boss is generous. How about you?"

"I'm in between jobs," Bryce said. "Since you're in tech you probably heard about the Bending shake up. I got shook out."

"I'm sorry to hear that!" India said. "That's the reason I started my own company. Got tired of these loopy white boys trying to be the next Bill Gates. So, what are your plans?"

"Not sure. The headhunters descended like vultures. I'm getting offers, but none where I'd like to be."

"Something will come up. If you worked for Bending, you're the G.O.A.T. You always have been."

A silence settled between them, both caught up in old memories. Bryce's phone buzzed.

"Shit, I got to get back."

They hugged again, this time more intimately.

"It was really good seeing you," India said.

"It was good seeing you, too," Bryce replied. He began walking away then stopped.

"Uh, India. Do you mind if I got your number? You being in tech and all, I might need a friendly reference."

India flashed a knowing grin. "Sure."

He gave her his phone and she entered it into his contacts.

"You can have mine too, if you want it."

"Sure!" she said.

Bryce texted her his number.

"So, you have a good Christmas," Bryce said.

A Palmetto Christmas

"You, too," India replied.

She leaned over, kissed his cheek, then walked away.

"Wow," Bryce said as he watched her leave. He finished his shopping then checked out. He halfway hoped he'd see her in the parking lot, but he didn't. It was just as well. The last thing he needed to be bothered with was illusions of an old girlfriend. Just another stress, and he was here to relax.

Shelly and Damian were waiting in the kitchen when he entered the house.

"What took you so long?" she asked.

"You won't believe it. I ran into India in the store."

Shelly's eyes went wide. "You're lying!"

"Who's India?" Damian asked.

"Bryce's summer love," Shelly said. "While the rest of us were having a good time, Bryce would be walking around holding hands with the island girl making googly eyes and who knows what else."

"Sounds like he was having a good time too, just in a different way," Damian replied.

"Listen to you!" Shelly said.

"It wasn't like that," Bryce said as he unbagged the groceries. "We were good friends. It was good seeing her. Brought back old memories."

"I bet," Shelly commented.

Laura entered the kitchen. "You finally made it back."

"Sorry it took a while. Ran into India at the grocery store."

"That cute little Gullah girl? You two were a pair. Y'all always managed to find each other no matter where we stayed."

"It's called a phone, Mama," Shelly said. "Bryce was giving her the 411 before we arrived."

"Actually, I wasn't," Bryce said. "It just always happened."

"Yeah, right," Shelly replied. "Anyway, I'm glad you're back. Damian and I are going to pick up the chewies then I'm giving him a tour of Sea Island."

"Take your jacket," Laura said. "It's a little chilly out there."

"Okay, Mama. See y'all in a few."

Bryce tossed Shelly the keys. She and Damian went on their way while Bryce put up the last of the groceries.

"Leave the sugar out, baby," Laura said. "I'm about to make cookies."

"But Shelly's picking up chewies," Bryce said.

"I know, but I want cookies, too. I know Mr. Sweet Tooth ain't complaining."

"I'm not as young as I used to be," Bryce said.

"Who you telling?" Laura replied. "It's the holidays. A few days of indulging ain't gonna hurt."

"Where's Pop and the kids?"

"Still running around on the beach."

"Let me go give him a break."

"No, you sit down right here," Laura said. "He'll be all right. All he does is sit in front of the television watching sports. He needs the exercise. And I need help with these cookies."

"Mama, you know I can't cook," Bryce said.

"I'm not asking you to cook. I'm going to need some help mixing. This dough gets thick at some point."

Bryce sat as he watched Mama take out the rest of the cookie ingredients.

"I talked to your daddy," Laura said. "I'm sorry about your job."

"Thanks, Mama. Things will work out."

"You know you and the kids are welcomed to come stay with us until you get things settled."

"I know, Mama, but it's not that bad. Like I told Pop, I received a severance that should keep me straight for at least six months."

"Still, if you need to, don't hesitate. You know we don't mind."

Bryce walked over to Mama and hugged her.

"Love you, Mama."

"Love you too, baby. Now hand me those chocolate chips."

"Why don't I just eat them?"

Laura smacked his shoulder.

"Quit playing, boy, and help."

Bryce brought over the chips and added them until Mama told him to stop. He took the mixing spoon from her and took over. Mama was right; it was tough. But nowhere near as tough as everything else. But it would all work out, one way or another.

-10-

Shelly steered the SUV off the major highway and onto the backroad leading to the old store. Damian leaned back in the passenger seat; his eyes closed. She grinned; he was cute when he slept.

"I could drive," he said, his eyes still closed.

"I'm good," Shelly replied. "Besides, I know my way around. It'll save us some time."

The store was open when they arrived. Miss Martha and Terrence were at the counter, waiting on a couple of early customers. Miss Martha saw her and waved.

"Terrence, get Miss Shelly her chewies," she said.

Terrence finished packing the other customers' bags then went to the back.

"So, how's the vacation going?" Miss Martha asked.

"Great," Shelly replied. "I came home to relax and that's exactly what I'm doing."

"That's what vacations are for," Miss Martha said. Her eyes narrowed when she looked at Damian.

"How you liking Sea Island?" she asked.

"It's beautiful and peaceful," Damian replied.

"It's gets a little busy around spring and summer. Y'all come at a good time. Not a lot of tourist attractions, and it can get mighty cold, but this is the best time for resting."

Terrence emerged from the back with two white boxes. He sat them on the counter and opened them. Inside were four plates of chewies. Shelly looked inside and her eyes went wide.

"Miss Martha, there are four trays of chewies in these boxes. I only ordered one."

Miss Martha grinned. "Grandma don't measure nothing. When she was done, she had enough for four."

Shelly wasn't prepared to pay for four plates. She took out her wallet but Damian stopped her.

"Let me get it this time," he said.

"Don't worry about it," Miss Martha said. "Pay me for the plate you ordered. The rest are on the house. Lord knows we ain't gonna eat all of them and you got a house full. Merry Christmas!"

"Are you sure?" Shelly asked. Miss Martha nodded.

"Damian, grab those boxes and let's go before this woman comes to her senses!"

Everyone laughed as Damian gathered the boxes. Shelly hugged Miss Martha and Terrence.

"Thank y'all so much!" she said. "Merry Christmas!"

"Merry Christmas to y'all, too!"

Damian loaded the chewies into the back seat then joined Shelly up front.

"Some real nice people around here," he said.

"They are," Shelly agreed "I'm gonna have to get both of them a present."

Damian frowned. "We're not going shopping, are we?"

"Not today," Shelly said. "Today you get a personal tour of Sea Island."

Shelly drove north to the bridge connecting the island to the mainland. Instead of crossing, she exited on a side road.

"This is one of my favorite spots," she said.

"What is it?" Damian asked.

"It's a bird sanctuary," Shelly replied. "Not many people come here. They're usually here for the beach. So many kinds of birds come during the spring and summer. I've never been during the winter, so I have no idea what we'll see."

"So, you're a nature girl," Damian said.

"Kind of," Shelly replied. "I like to be out in the woods, but I'm not the camping type. Too many critters. Besides, we do enough of that in this man's army."

They parked in the empty parking lot then walked the gravel trail into the sanctuary. The trees blocked the sunlight, cutting off what little warmth the winter sun shared. Damian pulled Shelly close.

"Somebody's getting cold," Shelly said.

"Not really," Damian replied.

The kiss was unexpected but welcomed. When it was over, Shelly tingled. It was far from their first kiss, but this one seemed more intimate.

"You had to be in the woods to kiss me like that?"

Damian grinned. "Couldn't find the right moment at the house. For such a big place somebody always seems to be around."

They walked hand in hand down the trail.

"That's my family. We like to be around each other. Always talking and laughing, especially this time of year. The fact that they're doing it around you means they like you."

"That's nice to hear," Damian said. "I'm still waiting for the interrogation from your father and brother."

"It's coming," Shelly replied. "You can count on it. I'm the baby. I need to be protected. Twenty-something years old and trained with weapons and I need to be protected."

"Annoying, huh?"

"Sometimes. Most of the time. I understand where it comes from, but still . . ."

"Don't be too hard on them. They care enough to be concerned. Not everybody gets that kind of love."

There was something in Damian's voice when he said those last words. Something personal.

"So have you contacted your family to let them know you're in the states?"

Damian looked away. "Not yet. I plan to."

"You thinking about going to see them?"

"I might." Damian squeezed her hand. "Right now, I'm exactly where I want to be."

Shelly felt he was done talking about his family. His business was his business, but she was curious to know why he would fly to the states to be with her and her family during the holidays but wouldn't take time to see his own.

"I thought you said this was a bird sanctuary," he said. "Haven't seen any so far."

"Maybe they're inside their nests sipping hot chocolate and watching bird sports," Shelly replied. "Let's pick up the pace. There's a marsh just beyond these trees. Maybe we'll see something there."

They hurried to the marsh and were rewarded with the sight of majestic blue herons and other wading birds searching the shallows for their next meals. They saw two osprey nests atop tall poles raised just for that purpose, although this time of year they were empty. Just before they returned to the SUV a lone bald eagle appeared, swooping down to the waters to grasp a hapless fish for a meal.

"You ready for that hot chocolate?" Shelly asked.

"I am," Damian answered.

"I know the perfect place."

She handed him the keys.

"You drive this time. I'll tell you what to do."

"Something tells me you like that," Damian teased.

Shelly punched his shoulder.

They left the sanctuary, Damian steering, Shelly directing. As she studied his face as he drove, she realized she was falling for him. Not in her usual way, but freefalling without any constraints. He was so patient, so polite, so attentive. But most men were in the beginning. How would he be six months, a year, three years from now? Who said their relationship would last that long? She shook her head. She was getting ahead of herself. Like Charlotte said, take it one day at a time. Reel in the doubts and let things play out naturally. Enjoy this time and let the future take care of itself.

"Am I going in the right direction?" Damian asked.

His question pulled her out of her musing.

"Actually, you missed the turn," she said.

"That's because I have a terrible copilot."

"Ha. Ha. Go up there, make a u-turn then a left at the next light."

Shelly's directions led them down a two-lane road that ended at a roundabout bordered by small shops and an amazing view of the marsh.

"Park there," Shelly said, pointing at a large lot to the left of the shops. They parked then strolled to a quaint coffee shop at the center of the buildings. A few people were inside, mainly older couples that came to the island in the winter to enjoy the properties they rented out during the busier seasons. The barista was a young, dark, brown-skinned man with an engaging smile.

"Welcome to NuBrews!" he said in a heavy Gullah accent. "What can I get you?"

"I'd like a mocha latte with honey," Shelly said.

The young man nodded. "And you sir?"
"Your strongest coffee. Black."
The barista nodded. "For here or to go?"
"For here," Shelly replied. "Want to enjoy that marsh view."
"It's beautiful, isn't it?" the barista said.
"Like everything else here," Damian replied, his eye on Shelly.

They waited by the counter while the barista made their coffee, then went to the outdoor patio with its expansive view of the marsh. They sipped their drinks, admiring the vista.

"So, tell me about yourself, Mr. Damian," Shelly said.

"Not much to tell," Damian replied. "Born and raised in Tulsa, graduated from high school, did a couple of years of college then joined the Air Force. And now I'm here."

"No sir, that is not enough," Shelly said. "That's your Wikipedia. I want all the details."

Damian took a sip of coffee. "Like I said, I was born in Tulsa. Nothing special . . . until my mom died."

"Oh no," Shelly said. She touched his hand. "I'm so sorry. What happened?"

"Car accident. She was on her way to work. I was ten. Me and Dad took it hard, of course. But he got over it sooner than I did."

Damian took another sip of coffee. "He remarried two years later. Maria. One of my mother's friends. She and her husband divorced a few years before Mama died. She had two children, a boy, and a girl a few years older than me. So, we all became one big happy family."

Shelly felt the sarcasm in his voice. "You don't have to talk about it if you don't want to."

"I do, actually," Damian said. "My dad worked so hard to make Maria and her kids feel accepted that he forgot about me. It was like he took me for granted. At first, I understood, but after a while it didn't make sense. It was like I became invisible. No matter how hard I tried, how good my grades were, I couldn't get his attention. And I don't even want to talk about Maria."

"I'm sorry," Shelly said again.

"You keep saying that. It's not your fault. It is what it is."

"Is that why you joined the Air Force?"

Damian nodded. "I wanted to get away. As far as I could. Since I couldn't afford to do it on my own, I did it on Uncle Sam's dime."

"When was the last time you visited your family . . . I mean your father?"

"I haven't been home since I left," Damian said.

"No news about him?"

"I heard he and Maria divorced a few years ago. Once he paid for her children's college, she was out."

"So, he's alone," Shelly said.

Damian looked at her. "That's his fault. What are you trying to say?"

"Nothing," Shelly said. "Come on, let's finish our drinks. I have something else to show you."

They finished their drinks then walked back to the SUV.

"Damian . . ."

"I know what you're thinking, and no."

"You sure?"

"I'm sure. He knows where I'm stationed. If he could contact me to tell me he was divorced, he could let me know he was sorry. But he hasn't."

Shelly grasped his arm then kissed his cheek.

"Well, just think about it. I'll go with you if it would help."

"Why would you do that?" Damian asked.

"Because sometimes doing tough things with someone supporting you makes it easier."

Damian shrugged. "So, what do you want to show me now?"

"A place that means a lot to me."

"Lead the way."

"I'll drive. You might get turned around. This spot is kinda difficult to get to."

Damian gave her the keys.

"I'm all yours," he said.

"Yes, you are," Shelly replied.

Shelly guided the vehicle back to the main road. She drove back to the northern part of the island.

"So, where we going?" Damian asked.

"A special place," she replied. "When the developers came to the island, they built the southern tip first because nobody lived there. It was marsh and swamp. The Gullah lived in the north, near the mainland. But as the land ran out on the southern tip, the developers started encroaching on Gullah land. There are some beaches and oceanside spots only the locals know about or frequent. On one of our visits a friendly server told my parents about this place."

Shelly turned down a two-lane road that faded away into a dirt road. She kept driving until the street ended. She parked in a clear spot then walked down a narrow trail that cut through a tangle of pines, oaks, and saw palmettos. The brush diminished, replaced by sand dunes topped with swaying sea oats. A thicket of wind-bent oaks rose before them, blocking the ocean view. When they emerged from the trees the beach was before them, the packed sand littered with a mix of driftwood of many sizes.

"Wow!" Damian said. "This is nice!"

"Isn't it?" Shelly said. "They call it Skeleton Beach because the wood is bleached white. Come on."

They walked to the sands then wandered through the stranded wood.

"We would come here and have picnics," Shelly said. "Me, Bryce, and Terry would play tag, hiding and climbing the woods with the local kids. This is where Bryce first met India. We had so much fun here."

"Let me take your picture," Damian asked.

Shelly found a large piece of driftwood then sat before the root ball. Damian took the picture with his phone.

"Okay, selfie time!" Shelly said.

Damian joined her and they took a few shots. She was putting her phone back into her pocket when it buzzed. She looked at the text message and her eyes went wide. She grabbed Damian's hand then began running back to the parking lot.

"Whoa!" Damian said. "What's wrong?"

"Nothing," Shelly said. "It's actually so right. Terry's here!"

A Palmetto Christmas

-II-

João turned the black convertible Mustang onto Palm Dunes parkway. He insisted they rent it just in case the weather was warm enough to let the top down. Once they reached Savannah, it was. Terry tied a stylish scarf around her hair, while João took off his hat to let the air blow against his head. The drive brought back so many memories, good and bad. Her stomach was in turmoil as they reached their destination.

They followed the weaving road deeper into the resort. People walked, jogged, and rode bikes along the paved trails on either side of the road, some of them sharing smiles and waves.

"Very nice people," João commented.

"You would be too if you could afford to own a house here."

"I could, actually," João replied. "You could, too."

"That's not the point," Terry said. "This is a lot of obscene wealth on display."

"You're not dragging me into an argument because you're nervous about seeing your family."

"That's not what I'm trying to do," Terry replied. Yet it was exactly what she was trying to do. Letting off a little steam by having a simple disagreement with João would be the perfect way to ease the pressure she felt. He wasn't going for it.

They stopped at the guard entrance. A woman in a blue security uniform looked at their dashboard then waved for them to pull over. After letting a few cars through, she walked to them.

"How y'all doing?" she said.

"Fine," Terry replied. "Is there a problem?"

"Yes. Cars aren't allowed beyond this point without a parking permit."

"Oh," Terry said. "We don't have one. We're here visiting my parents. They've rented a house for the holidays."

The guard frowned. "They should have purchased an additional parking pass and sent it to you."

"They didn't know we were coming. It's a surprise."

"What's their names?" the guard asked.

"Laura and Stanley Jacobs."

"And their address?"

143 Seashore Lane."

The guard walked back to the booth, then returned a few minutes later.

"I'll let you through this time," she said. "But make sure you get a parking pass if you're going to be in and out."

"Thank you. We will," Terry said.

The guard lifted the gate and they continued into the resort.

"They take security seriously here," João commented.

"They do, which is a good thing."

Seashore Lane ran parallel to the beach, the view blocked by huge stucco homes and immaculate landscaping. Terry was pleasantly surprised Mama and Daddy finally decided to splurge a bit. She remembered the tight times growing up. Being the oldest, she wasn't sheltered from the hard work both had to do to keep the family stable. She helped Mama make cakes she would sell at church and at her job, and Daddy would call her outside to help repair their car. Things changed when Daddy got hired at Madison Bakery. It was a job that paid well with good benefits. She spent so much of her childhood doing what she had to do. That was why she went to college. She was determined to do what she wanted to do.

"We're here!" João announced.

He steered into the driveway of a handsome home.

"Here we go," Terry said.

João kissed her cheek. "Everything will be fine. It's the holidays!"

Terry cut her eyes at João. "We'll see. I'm not staying where I'm not wanted. Be ready to leave."

"You don't have faith in good outcomes," João said.

"I do, but I know my parents."

They exited the car then walked up to the door. Terry stood still, staring at the doorbell button.

"Oh, for goodness sake!" João said. He pressed the button.

"Who in the world?" said a woman. The door opened and Terry stood face to face with Mama.

"Terry? Oh, sweet Jesus! Terry!"

Mama grabbed her around the neck and pulled her into a tight hug. Terry hugged Mama back, all the apprehension melting away in an embrace she didn't realize she missed so much.

"It's me, Mama," she whispered.

"Stanley! Bryce!" Laura shouted. "Terry's here!"

Terry looked up and saw Daddy and Bryce running to the door.

"Terry!" Stanley said. He joined in the hug. Bryce stood back, folding his arms across his chest and smirking.

"About damn time," he said. His children appeared, grabbing his legs.

"Daddy, who is that?" Constance asked.
"That's your Aunt Terry," Bryce answered.
"Did she bring any candy?" Cameron asked.
"No," Bryce replied.
"Okay," Cameron said before walking away.
Terry laughed.
"Just like his daddy," she said.
Terry eased away from Mama and Daddy and hugged Bryce.
"How's my little brother?"
"I'm good, big sister."
"Ahem!"
Everyone turned to João, who stood with his hands behind his back, an expectant look on his face.
"Y'all, this is my boyfriend, João Rebeiro."
"Wait a minute," Laura said. She studied João's face then covered her mouth with her hands.
"João Rebeiro from The Traveling Chef! I watch your show on the Food Channel!"
"Guilty as charged," João confessed.
"Y'all come on in!" Laura said. "Bryce, text Shelly and tell her to get her butt back to the house!"
Laura stepped inside the foyer.
"I'll get our luggage," João said. "You go on."
Terry let Mama lead her to the huge family room. They sat on the recliner sofa, Mama on one side, Daddy on the other. It felt comforting and awkward to have them both so close physically when she knew mentally, they were so far apart.
"You look good, Baby," Laura said.
"Y'all do, too," Terry replied.
"For our age," Laura said. "We're barely hanging in there."
"Speak for yourself," Stanley replied. "So how you doing?"

"I'm fine, Daddy," Terry said, bracing herself for what was coming next.

"You still drawing?" he asked.

"I'm an artist," Terry replied.

"And an amazing one at that!"

João entered the family room, putting down the luggage. "Terry is one of the best artists in the world. And I'm not just saying that because I love her. I met her at a showing in Toronto and was blown away by her work."

"He loved my art, and I loved his food," Terry said.

Someone screamed outside.

Daddy stood up. "What in the . . ."

The front door swung open and Shelly ran inside. "Terry!"

Terry stood just in time to catch her sister and fall back onto the couch. Laura and Stanley moved out of the way as fast as they could as the two of them tumbled to the floor.

"Girl! You too big for this!" Terry scolded before laughing.

"I know you told me you were coming, but I refused to believe it until I saw you."

"You knew she was coming?" Laura said.

Terry and Shelly clambered from the floor.

"Yes," Shelly replied. "I didn't tell y'all because I didn't want y'all to have time to catch an attitude."

Laura and Stanley looked at each other then nodded.

"We're all here now," Laura said. "A good holiday just became a great holiday. Stanley, show João to his and Terry's room."

"Wait," Shelly said. "They get to stay in a room together?"

"Don't start with me, Shelly," Laura warned.

Shelly threw up her hands. "Anyway, we picked up the chewies, but we're missing one important thing."

"What's that?" Bryce asked.

"A Christmas tree!"

"Baby, we decided we didn't want to do all that here," Laura said.

"That's when it was just you and Daddy," Shelly replied. We got the whole family here, including the babies. We have to have a tree!"

"I came down here so I wouldn't have to fuss with a tree," Stanley said. "You're on your own."

"And what about lights?" Laura asked. "What you gonna do about lights?"

"We'll buy them!" João said.

Laura sat beside Stanley. Both pretended not to care, but it was hard for them to keep from smiling.

"Y'all do what you want. We'll be right here relaxing," Stanley said.

"So, y'all want to do this?" Shelly asked.

Terry, João, Damian, Bryce, and the kids all nodded. Shelly clapped her hands.

"Then let's go!'

Bryce took the kids to their room and got their jackets. João and Terry put away their things then everyone gathered in the foyer.

"See y'all later!" Shelly said. She led everyone out of the house.

* * *

Laura and Stanley stared at the door for a moment longer before walking back to the kitchen.

"Not the relaxing vacation you expected, is it?" Stanley said.

"We're retired," Laura replied. "We relax all the time. I'd rather have a busy house with my family than a quiet house alone."

"Oh, so I'm invisible?"

Laura laughed. "You know what I'm talking about."

Stanley tickled Laura. "No, I don't."

"Stop, boy!" Laura said.

"So, I'm a boy now, too!"

"When you act like one."

Laura opened one of the boxes of chewies. "Did you bring that dessert wine we got at Frogtown Cellars?"

"Yes, I did."

Let's go sit on the patio and eat in peace."

Stanley ambled to their room then returned with the narrow bottle of sweet muscadine wine.

"I thought you said you liked a busy house."

"I do, but not all the time."

She kissed Stanley before he could say another word.

"Come on, boy. Let's eat."

Stanley smiled. "Lead the way!"

-12-

The short trip to find a Christmas tree became an excursion. There were no tree farms on the island, so the family set out for the mainland. They searched the farms in Bluffton, but the choices were scarce since they were looking at the last minute. The owner of the last farm they checked told them there was a farm near Beaufort that was pick and cut down your own tree, so that's where the family headed.

"There it is!" Shelly said as she pointed.

"Hands on the wheel," Bryce replied.

Shelly cut her eyes at her brother then guided the SUV to the small parking lot. Bryce unbuckled the kids then unleashed them onto the grounds. They ran into the rows of trees with wide eyes. The grown-ups took their time, walking up to the outside counter.

"I smell hot chocolate," Terry said.

"Me, too," João replied.

The owner, a jovial-looking fellow with red cheeks wearing a red flannel shirt, brown lederhosen, and an elf hat grinned as he waved them over.

"Merry Christmas!" he said.

"Merry Christmas!" they replied.

"I'm Charley the Tree Man. We have hot chocolate and coffee. Take your pick."

Terry, Shelly, and João made a beeline to the hot chocolate. Bryce fixed himself a coffee.

"Let me find my children before they break something," he said.

"It's fine," Charley replied. "My trees are as sturdy as they come."

"You don't know my kids," Bryce said.

Bryce and Charley strolled to the trees.

"I'm coming too!" João said. "Terry?"

"I'll be along," Terry replied.

Damian looked at Shelly, then Terry.

"I think you two need time to talk," he said. "I'll go with the boys."

Shelly answered him with a smile. She waited until the men disappeared into the trees before grabbing Terry's arm and pulling her away.

"So, you brought him home!" Shelly said.

"So did you," Terry replied. "Don't you think that's kind of soon?"

Shelly looked thoughtful. "Yeah, and no. Charlotte said I should go for it."

"You listened to Charlotte?" Terry rolled her eyes. "From what you've told me about her, she might not be the best source of advice."

"She is a little fast," Shelly admitted.

"A little? That woman is a Ferrari."

"Well, things seem to be working out so far," Shelly said. "He's a little quiet about his family, but he's so nice."

"They all are in the beginning. Let's see how he is six months from now."

Shelly stared at Terry. "You act like I ain't never had a man before."

Terry's expression softened and she hugged Shelly.

"I'm sorry. I'm just looking out for you."

"Always being big sister," Shelly replied. "But I had to do something different. Nothing else has worked out. I really like Damian, and I know he likes me. He didn't have to come but he did. And he's been quite the gentleman the entire time."

"That's good, Shay-Shay," Terry said, using her nickname for her baby sister. "But you know how you are. You love hard and you hurt deeply. Be careful."

"I will. But what's up with you and João? Y'all been together for a minute."

"Five years," Terry said.

"No talk of wedding bells?"

Terry shrugged. "Not really."

"And that doesn't bother you?"

Terry shrugged. "If it happens, it happens. If it doesn't, it doesn't."

"You don't really believe that do you?"

"I do," Terry said. Me and João have a good thing. If it stays just like this, I won't complain. And I'm definitely not mentioning marriage. That's a conversation that if the timing's not right it can ruin everything."

"I don't see how," Shelly said.

"Because if one or the other is not ready, the relationship is over," Terry said. "I mean, how do you go back to normal after that?"

"But what if he asked you right now?" Shelly asked. "Would you accept?"

Terry looked away. "I don't know. I really don't know."

Their conversation was interrupted by their niece and nephew running toward them with bright faces.

"Auntie Terry! Auntie Shelly!" Constance shouted. "Come see our tree!"

"Our tree!" Cameron repeated.

She grabbed both their hands and tugged them toward the artificial grove. Terry and Shelly followed them to where Damian, João, and Bryce stood watching the owner cut down the seven-foot Fraser fir.

"Woo, that's a tall one!" Terry said.

"A big tree for a big house," Bryce replied.

"How we gonna get it to the house?" Damian asked.

"We'll deliver it," Charley replied. "Whereabouts y'all live?"

"We're vacationing at Palmetto Marsh," Shelly said.

"I know where that is. We deliver there all the time," Charley said. "All I need is the address and we'll have it there by the end of the day. The guards know us, so we won't need a pass."

"Cool," Bryce said. "Then we'll pay and be on our way."

Charley finished cutting down the tree then let his helpers handle the rest. Bryce was about to pay when Terry stepped in.

"Let me," she said. "You need to save your pennies."

"I'm good," Bryce replied. "It'll be a few months before I'll need a handout."

They laughed.

"Still, I'm big sister," Terry said.

"Here you are, Charley," João said. He gave Charley his card. Charley smiled at Terry and Bryce.

"Problem solved," he said.

"Okay everybody!" Shelly announced. "Let's head back!"

"Awwwwww," the children said.

"Awwwwww," João repeated.

"Stop, boy," Terry said.

"But I want to see more of this beautiful island," João fussed. "It would be nice to stop by a local market as well."

"I know what you want to do," Terry said. "And that's a no. This is Mama's time to shine."

"I had no intentions of intruding on her culinary space," João replied. "As a matter of fact, I'm hoping to pick up a few tips. I've always been intrigued by southern American cooking. And we're in the famous Low Country, too? This is perfect."

Terry rolled her eyes. "You say that every time. Next thing you know I'm sitting by myself and you're clanging pots and pans and reveling everyone with your stories."

"What's wrong with that?" Bryce said. "I was kinda looking forward to it."

"How about a compromise?" Shelly said. "Let's ride over to Savannah tomorrow and hit some of their restaurants. I think some of your colleagues have visited some of them. You probably know a few of them."

"They have and I do!" João said. "Maybe we can visit them as well!"

"We're only here for a few days, remember?" Terry said.

"I wouldn't mind if we stayed a few more days, maybe until New Year's?"

Terry frowned. "That depends. Can I speak to you for a minute?"

João followed Terry until they were distant from the others.

"Look, you need to slow down," she said. "Things aren't right between me and my parents yet."

"Oh," João replied. "Everything seems fine to me."

"That's because they're in front of you," Terry replied. "We haven't had the behind closed doors conversation yet."

"And when will that happen?"

A Palmetto Christmas

Tery looked at her feet. "I don't know."

João put his arm around her shoulders and she hugged his waist.

"Don't wait," he said. "It's best to get these sorts of things out in the open as soon as possible."

"You don't understand," Terry said.

"I don't," João confessed. "I do know that we only have so many years in this world, and we should spend them as joyfully as we can. If you can't find joy here, then we should leave. But I have a feeling that things are not as serious as you think."

Terry hugged João tighter. "I hope you're right."

"Let's go back before everyone thinks we're fighting," João said. "I don't want to give your father and brother any reason to think less of me."

Terry rolled her eyes. "It's always all about you."

"And you, meu amor," João replied.

They returned to the group. Shelly eyed them then smirked. "Anybody hungry?" she asked.

The kids raised their hands.

"I could use a bite," Damian said.

"Me too," Bryce agreed.

"I'm heard there's a great Gullah restaurant on St. Helena Island." She jumped onto her phone searching for the location. "Here it is! Low Country Grill. We're not far so let's check it out!" Shelly said.

They piled into the SUV and set out for the island. They found the restaurant and had a hearty lunch then headed back to the resort. They arrived with the tree delivery service.

Shelly knocked on the door and Stanley answered.

"Where y'all been?" he said. "I know it didn't take that long to find a tree."

"It didn't," Bryce said. "Your daughter decided she wanted to be a tour guide."

Shelly laughed. "I didn't hear you complaining while you were stuffing your mouth with fish and grits."

"My mouth was full," Bryce said.

"Y'all come on in," Stanley said.

They entered the house then made room for the tree. The delivery truck arrived a few minutes later. Laura met them in the foyer.

"Y'all follow me," she said. She led them to the family room.

"Right here." Laura pointed to the spot they cleared for the tree. "I hope you brought a tree stand, because we don't have one."

"No lights either," Stanley said.

"We did," one of the men said. "We'll set it up, no charge."

"We'll get the lights later," Shelly said. "Me, Mama, and Terry. In fact, let's go right now. We'll take the kids with us and give the men a chance to talk."

"I think that's a great idea!" Laura agreed.

Terry cut her eyes at Shelly, and Shelly answered with a mischievous grin. Damian touched her shoulder.

"I'd rather go with y'all," he said.

"It's okay," Shelly replied. "Daddy is cool."

"It's not that," he said. "Can we talk a minute?"

Shelly looked puzzled. "Okay."

Shelly followed Damian outside.

"Look, I appreciate you inviting me here," he said. "You're amazing, and your family is great. But I need a little space."

"Space? What do you mean? What's wrong?"

"It's not y'all. It's me. Things are a little too close too fast."

Shelly took a step back. "Are you leaving?"

Damian took Shelly's hand. "No, I'm not leaving. I love it here. But I'm gonna check into a hotel. I'll come through when there's a gathering, and you can come see me."

"This is awkward, Damian," Shelly said. "If this is my fault, please say it. I can be a little fast when I meet someone I really like. Like you."

Damian leaned forward and they kissed.

"Like I said, it's not you. It's me."

"Can we talk about it?"

"Maybe, but not now."

Shelly was a tempest of emotions. She stared at Damian, not knowing what to do or say next.

"Maybe you could get your brother to run me to the Marriott? It's on the property, and they have rooms available."

"So, you've been thinking about this for a while."

Damian looked away.

"Okay, cool," Shelly said. "I bet your stuff is already packed, too."

"Ah, yeah."

Shelly turned then walked away, her confusion giving way to anger.

"Stay out here," she said.

Everyone was still near when she came inside.

"You ready?" Mama asked.

Shelly didn't reply. She went to Damian's room then opened his closet. She took out his packed bags then returned to the foyer. Terry and Bryce stepped forward.

"What a minute, what's going on?" Bryce asked.

"Damian has decided to stay in a hotel," Shelly said.

"What?!?" Terry exclaimed.

Stanley walked up with a smile.

"About time somebody in this house showed some respect." He cut his eye at João.

"Have I done something wrong?" João asked.

"Can you drive him to the Marriott?" Shelly asked Bryce. "It's on the property."

Bryce's eyes narrowed. "Sure. I'll take him."

"Don't mess with him, Bryce. I mean it. It's complicated."

"Whatever you say, baby sister," Bryce replied.

"I'll go," João said. "Seems like I might have to get a room, too."

Terry's eyes went wide. "You don't have to do that," she said. "You're my guest!"

"And you're all our guests," Laura chimed in. "Let me go talk to that boy."

"No, Mama," Shelly said. "Please don't. It's bad enough."

Shelly handed Bryce the keys.

"We'll be back in a few," he said. He and João walked out the door.

* * *

As soon as the door shut Bryce rushed up to Damian. Damian threw up his hands.

"Hold up, bruh!"

"What did you do to my sister?" Bryce said. He was about to get in Damian's face when João grabbed his arm. Bryce tried to jerk away, but João's grip was firm.

"Bryce," he said. "Let him explain."

"Can we get in the car and go first?" Damian asked.

"Yeah, let's do that," Bryce said. "You sit next to me."

"No," João said. "Damian, you sit in the back. I'll take shotgun."

They climbed into the SUV. Bryce put the hotel into the GPS.

"It's not far," Damian replied.

Bryce looked into the review mirror. "So, you need to start explaining now."

"I had no intentions of coming here," Damian said. "I usually knock around Europe for the holidays. I was planning to go to France and Spain. Then Shelly invited me to come here with her."

"Why did you accept?" Bryce asked.

"Because I like her. A lot. I was surprised she asked me. She seemed so reserved, then suddenly, she asked me to come with her."

"So, you changed your mind now," Bryce said.

"Yes . . . no . . . shit, I don't know. But it's not because of Shelly. Being around your family is a lot."

"What do you mean by 'a lot'?"

"My family situation ain't that great," Damian said. "It's the reason I joined the Air Force, and it's the reason I don't go home for Christmas. But being around y'all, and seeing what y'all have . . ."

"I understand," João said.

Bryce took a quick glance at João then turned his attention back to the road.

"Do you now?"

João nodded. "I do. My family was dirt poor. We had less than nothing, but we did have love. When I finally became a successful chef, I made sure my family was successful, too. I moved them out of the favelas and now they have all the things they wanted. But it didn't change our love."

"What does that have to do with Damian?"

"For a while I felt like him," João said. "But I learned to embrace love wherever I found it."

João turned around in his seat and smiled at Damian.

"You need to learn that, too. Shelly would be a great teacher."

"We're here," Bryce said.

Bryce steered the SUV into the Marriot roundabout. The valet met them as they pulled into the drop-off.

"Welcome to the Marriott," the man said with a smile. "I'm Lawrence. Let me get your bags."

"I'm good," Damian said. "Don't worry. I'll still tip you."

Lawrence tipped his hat. "Let me know if you need anything. Enjoy your stay at the Marriott."

He strolled back to the valet stand. Bryce and João helped Damian get his bags then carried them into the lobby. They waited while he checked in. Damian walked up to Bryce and extended his hand. Bryce glanced at it then back at Damian.

"Look bruh, I figure what you got going on has nothing to do with Shelly and how you feel about her. That's cool. But you need to make that clear to her. She's coming out of a bad relationship and she has a lot of doubts. I don't know where y'all are going with this but be honest with her. Okay?"

"I will," Damian said. "We still cool?"

"I'm Shelly's big brother. We'll never be completely cool. Just make sure you do right by her."

"Bryce!"

Bryce flinched. João and Damian looked behind him.

"Who is this?" João asked.

Bryce knew before he turned around. When he did, he saw April walking toward him, a big smile on her face.

"It's April. My ex," he said.

"I thought you lived in Chicago?" Damian said.

"I do."

"Then what is she doing here?" João asked.

"I have no idea. But I'm about to find out. Can y'all give me a few minutes?"

"Of course," João said. I'm going to explore this hotel."

"I'm going to my room," Damian said. "Good luck."

"Yeah, right," Bryce replied.

April walked up to him, her arms open. Bryce held up his hand then shook his head. He was not happy.

"What are you doing here?" he asked.

April's smile faded.

"I thought you'd be happy to see me," she said.

"Why?" he asked.

"Come on, Bryce. Don't be that way. It's Christmas."

"The last time we spoke, you were on your way to Costa Rica," he said.

April looked away. "Yeah, about that. The trip was cancelled. Nelson had a last-minute business obligation. He'll be back on Christmas eve."

"This is my holiday with the kids," Bryce said. "My entire family is here. It's been years since that's happened. I plan to spend it quietly . . . without you."

April smirked. "You say that, but you don't mean it."

Bryce rolled his eyes. "April, what are you trying to do? I got too much shit going on than to be dealing with you right now."

"I don't want to be alone," April said. "I want to spend time with my children . . . and you."

Bryce was speechless for a moment. He still had feelings for April and she knew it. His anger was his way of covering his emotions and keeping her at bay. It took him a minute to gather himself.

"Look, I'm not going to be your rebound when your little boyfriend doesn't have time for you. We were married. It's all or nothing. And right now, it's nothing."

"It could be different," April said.

"What are you talking about?"

"I've been thinking. We need to talk."

"Don't do this, April. Not now. If you have anything to say it can wait until after the holidays."

"No. It can't."

João sauntered up then stood beside Bryce.

"Hi. I'm João, Terry's boyfriend. And you are April."

"Yes, I am," April said. She extended her hand; João took it then pulled her into a hug.

"Nice to meet you," he said.

"Wow. You're friendly." April's eyes shifted to Bryce. "So, Terry's here?"

"Like I said, the whole family is here," Bryce replied.

"Tell her I said hello."

"Come on, João."

Bryce started for the door, then suddenly turned around.

"Don't let the kids know you're here," he said.

"I won't, until you tell me otherwise," April replied.

Bryce frowned at her then stormed out of the hotel. João had to run to catch up with him. They climbed into the SUV; Bryce started the vehicle then just sat there gripping the wheel.

A Palmetto Christmas

"I guess we should go back now?" João asked. "Shelly and your mother are waiting."

"Right."

Bryce pulled away.

"I don't know your situation, but maybe April coming here is a good thing," João said.

"Like you said, you don't know our situation," Bryce replied. "April is selfish and used to getting what she wants. If she thinks she can just pop down here and get her way, she's about to learn differently."

"Are you saying this because you're angry, or is there something else?"

Bryce stopped the SUV.

"Look bruh, I don't know you, and you don't know me. The last thing I need right now is some Google psychologist trying to analyze a situation they know nothing about. So, save your opinions for you and Terry. Okay?"

"Okay," João said. "I'll leave you be."

By the time they returned to the house, Bryce was seething. Shelly met them at the door then immediately stepped back.

"Brother, what's wrong?"

"I can't talk about it right now," he answered.

"Daddy!"

The sight of the kids took him down a bit.

"Hey! Y'all want to walk on the beach?"

"Yea!" the replied.

"Come on let's get your jackets."

Laura stopped him before he could follow them to the room.

"What's going on, Bryce?"

"April's here."

Laura's eyes went wide.

"What? Oh, my goodness! Why?"

"I don't want to talk about it, okay?" he said, his voice raised.

"Oh shit," Terry said.

Bryce went into the room and helped the kids into their jackets. When they came out, everyone stared at them.

"We'll be back in a few," he said.

They went out the back sliding door, the children running across the patio to the wooden walkway that cut through the sea oats and sand dunes to the beach. The combination of sea mist and wind made it feel chillier than it was, but Bryce didn't care. He needed to cool down. He would have to keep an eye on the kids, though. Children don't realize they're cold until it's too late.

"Stay out of the water!" he yelled.

They yelled back.

Bryce watched them play, getting as close as they could to the waves then looking back at him to see if he was paying attention. Then they began searching for seashells. Bryce's thoughts drifted back to when he was their age. The beach was so fascinating to him; just watching the waves move back and forth was enough.

"Hey, Bryce."

He turned to see Terry and Shelly coming toward him. They both hugged him and he smiled.

"So, what the hell is April doing here?" Terry asked.

"Her boy toy stood her up, so she decided to come down here and make my life miserable."

"For real?" Shelly asked.

"She says she's been thinking about us."

"You don't believe her, do you?"

Bryce shrugged.

Terry threw her hands up. "Come on, Bryce! You're about as bad as Shelly."

"Hey!" Shelly said.

"You know I'm right," Terry said. "Y'all fall in love at the drop of a hat."

"You forget April and I were married for ten years," Bryce said. "You don't get over something like that, just like that."

"Plus, the kids," Shelly added.

"By the way, your boyfriend talks too much," Bryce said.

"He does," Terry agreed. "I think it's that Latin macho thing. He has an answer for everything and everyone."

"So now we know why you're not in love," Shelly said.

"I am . . . I think," Terry said.

"You think?" Bryce asked.

"It never came up," Terry said. "We met five years ago and have been together since. I've never told him I love him, and he's never said it to me, at least not directly. Which is cool."

"Is it?"

"Look, we aren't talking about me," Terry said. "What you gonna do, Bryce?"

"I'm gonna watch my kids play on this cold beach," he said.

"But you need to decide," Shelly said.

"No, I don't," Bryce replied. "April knows we're in Palmetto Marsh but she doesn't know which house. And even if she finds out, I'm sure she won't come over unless I say she can."

"She flew from Chicago," Terry said. "She's probably online searching for clues."

"If it was just me, I would agree," Bryce said. "But whatever she does, she won't do it in front of the kids. We agreed to keep our business between us."

A strong wind gust dropped the temperature and it drizzled. It was so chilly the kids felt it despite their winter clothes. They squealed then ran to the adults.

"Daddy, I'm cold!" Constance shouted.

"My butt is freezing!" Cameron screamed.

Terry, Bryce, and Shelly laughed. Terry squatted down and Constance outran her little brother to their daddy's embrace. Cameron's bottom lip had started to tremble when Shelly scooped him up into her arms.

"Now I know you're not gonna start crying because Aunt Shelly picked you up?"

"I want daddy!" he fussed.

"Why?" Shelly asked.

"Because he's warmer than you," Cameron replied.

Shelly chuckled. "He's Bryce's boy all right. Spoiled as ever."

Shelly walked over to Bryce.

"Here. Take your boy," she said. Bryce laughed as he took Cameron. Constance reached out for Shelly.

"Auntie Shelly! You can carry me!"

Shelly took Constance.

"Now this girl had good sense," Shelly commented.

"Y'all quit playing and come on. The rain is getting heavy," Terry said.

The rain came down hard as they reached the dunes. They were soaked as they entered the house."

"No, you don't!" Laura said. "Don't y'all track all that water and sand into my house! Y'all stay right there."

"This isn't your house, Mama," Terry said with a smirk.

"It is if I'm here," Laura replied. "Stanley, go get them some towels."

Stanley grunted as he pushed himself up from the comfortable lounger. "You know we came here to relax, right?"

Laura gave him a mean stare and he raised his hands.

"Alright, alright. My goodness." Stanley shuffled out of the family room then returned with towels.

"And leave them shoes by the door," Laura added.

"Yep, we're definitely in Laura Moreland's house," Shelly whispered.

"I heard that," Laura said. "Don't be using my maiden name in vain."

Bryce, Terry, and Shelly laughed. Bryce dried off the kids then sent them to their room to change clothes.

"You still want to go get those decorations, Shelly?" Bryce asked.

"Of course! But I understand if you don't feel like it."

"Let's go. I need the distraction. Mama, you mind watching the kids while we're gone?"

"Not at all," Laura said. "Always got time for my grandbabies."

"Terry, you coming?" Bryce asked.

"No, I'm staying here," she said. "I don't want to leave João alone with anybody too long."

"Bring him," Shelly said.

"Not a good idea. Whatever you're planning to do, it takes twice as long with João."

João strolled into the foyer. "I'm not that bad."

"Really?" Terry replied.

"I can't help it if I'm meticulous," João said. "That's why I'm a great chef!"

"Yes, you are, baby," Terry said. She kissed his cheek. "But you're staying here with me."

"Good! I can ask your mother and father all about little Terry."

Terry rolled her eyes. "Y'all go ahead. We'll catch you on the way in."

Shelly and Bryce went to the SUV then were on their way to the department store.

"It's kind of late to be hunting from Christmas decorations," Bryce said. "Probably won't have much to choose from."

"We'll make do," Shelly replied. "Christmas ain't Christmas without lights."

"So, what you gonna do about Damian?" Bryce asked.

"I don't know," Shelly said. "This was a bad idea. I shouldn't have asked him to come."

"He wouldn't be here if he didn't want to be," Bryce said.

"Maybe he was just being nice," Shelly said.

"No man is going to fly to another continent with somebody because he's nice," Bryce said. "He likes you a lot. He's got something else going on. You should talk to him."

"I'll give him a call," Shelly said. "I'm trying to give him some space."

"Don't give him too much," Bryce replied.

They pulled into the Martway parking lot. It was packed with shoppers getting in the last-minute shopping from the big day. Bryce followed Shelly into the store.

"Come on, I know where the decorations are," Shelly said.

They were about to walk down the main aisle when Bryce stopped, his eyes focused on the grocery section. Standing over the collards greens was India. She wore jeans and a loose sweater, and a headwrap covering her locs.

Is that India?" Shelly asked.

Bryce smiled. "It is."

"She looks good!"

"She does," Bryce replied. "You go ahead," Bryce said. "I'll catch up."

Shelly chuckled. "Yeah, right. I'll meet you back at the car."

"I won't be that long," Bryce replied. "I'm just gonna speak."

"Whatever, brother."

Shelly hurried away. Bryce sauntered over to India.

"We have to stop meeting like this," he said.

India turned and smiled.

"Something about us and groceries," she replied.

"We always had a way of finding each other, even when we weren't looking."

India's smile widened. "What are you doing here?"

"Shelly decided we needed a Christmas tree and lights, so here we are."

India looked around him. "Shelly's here? I haven't seen her in ages!"

"You should come by the house," Bryce said. "Mama and Daddy would love to see you."

"I couldn't," India replied. "I don't want to intrude on your family gathering."

"I'm inviting you," Bryce said. "I'll text you the address. You can decide later."

"I'll think about it. Now let me get back to picking these greens," India said. "Mama's waiting."

"And I need to find Shelly. See you later?"

India smirked. "Maybe."

Bryce bounced down the aisle in search of Shelly. India had a way of making him feel lighter, even back in the day when they spent time on the beach. For that brief moment April never came to mind, but as he found Shelly he was brooding again.

Shelly was shoveling lights and other decorations into her buggy.

"Hold up!" Bryce said. "Looks like you're buying enough lights for the whole island."

Shelly stuck out her tongue. "I'm getting enough so we can decide what we like. Whatever we don't want we can bring back."

"Why don't you just take pictures and text them," Bryce said.

"It's not the same," Shelly replied. "Can't wait till Mama sees this." Shelly looked over his shoulder. "Where's India?"

"Picking out greens," Bryce said.

"You didn't bring her with you?"

"Why?"

"So, I can speak to her! God, you're so impolite!"

Shelly almost ran into him as she hurried down the aisle to the produce section. By the time they reached it, India was gone. Bryce did a quick scan of the checkout lanes and didn't see her. To his surprise, he was disappointed.

"I guess she's gone," he said. "She said she was in a hurry."

"Shoot! I wanted to say hi. It's been years. I guess I'll have to wait until the next time."

"What next time?" Bryce asked.

Shelly sucked her teeth as she hunted for the shortest checkout line.

"Like you didn't get her number."

"I didn't," Bryce said.

"Cap."

"Well, yeah I did, but not the way you're thinking."

Shelly rolled her eyes. "Come on, boy. We need to get these lights up and give your children a proper Christmas."

Bryce and Shelly meandered through the crowded lot back to the SUV. They loaded quickly then got inside.

"It's okay, you know," Shelly said.

"What?"

She turned to her brother as he started the car.

"It's okay for you to call India. You need to start living your life again."

"I don't need your permission, little sis. And I wish it were that easy. In addition to raising these kids, I have to find a job. I don't have the time, especially for someone a thousand miles away."

"And you still love April," Shelly added.

"What are you talking about?"

"You still love her; despite all the shit she's dragged you through. But she's always been good at that."

Bryce stopped the SUV.

"Hold up. I know you ain't talking. Remember Sam?"

Shelly closed her eyes and took a deep breath.

"Of course I do. That's why I know you still love April. And you need to start back driving."

Bryce looked around and saw the line of impatient drivers growing behind him. He sped away from the light.

"It's like I said. Y'all ain't never been married. Your feelings just don't end like that, even if the other partner is to blame."

Shelly leaned over and gave Bryce a one-armed hug. Bryce hugged her back.

"Ain't we two something?" he said.

"But let's put that all away," Shelly said. "We're here with our whole family, the first time in a long time. Let's enjoy that."

"I agree," Bryce said.

"So, let's get back so we can put these ugly lights on the tree."

Bryce laughed. "You said it. I didn't."

-13-

Terry couldn't sleep. It was never a problem before with João, but that night she was on edge. They were two of a kind, always getting along and rarely arguing. Terry credited that to their honest relationship. They never hid anything from each other, no matter how silly or embarrassing. It was a different relationship, light years away from her parents.

But did she love him? And did he love her?

"Stupid Bryce," she whispered. "This is your fault."

She eased out of bed, put on her housecoat then headed for the fridge. She wasn't hungry, but a craving is a craving. She hoped there was peanut butter.

She crept from the room and into the hallway. The kitchen light was on; someone else was probably awake. She started to go back to bed, not sure if she wanted to share a quiet moment with anyone else. She shrugged and continued. It was probably Bryce or Shelly. The two were notorious for their late-night refrigerator raids, at least when they were kids.

As she neared the kitchen, she heard singing. Terry hurried into the kitchen, knowing who she would see. Laura sat at the table, singing with her eyes closed.

"Mama?"

Laura jumped. Her shocked look transformed into a smile.

"Terry, what you doing up this early?"

"I can ask you the same question," Terry said.

"Just getting my quiet time in before the day started," Laura said.

Terry sat down. "I guess we ruined your peaceful vacation."

"No, baby, not at all," Laura replied. "You know how long it's been since the last time we had all y'all together?"

"Five years at least," Terry said. "That was the last time I came home."

"That long," Laura said.

There was a moment of silence before Laura spoke again. "I guess you're here for the peanut butter."

Terry grinned.

"It's in the cabinet. Got some just for you."

Terry skipped to the cabinet then took out the peanut butter. She was reaching for the bread when she stopped.

"Wait a minute. You knew I was coming?"

"I hoped. I know you and Shelly talk, and I know she told you we were getting together."

"I have to keep up with baby sister," she replied. Terry grabbed a butter knife from the drawer, a plate from the cabinet and bread. She sat down and began spreading the peanut butter on the end slice. Laura shook her head.

"The only person I know that eats the end slice of the bread."

Terry grinned. "Besides you."

"João seems nice."

"He is."

"Y'all making any plans?"

"For what?"

"Girl, you know what I'm talking about."

Terry bit into her peanut butter sandwich. It was delicious. Much better than the peanut butter in Canada.

"We're taking it one day at a time."

"Five years is a lot of days."

Terry closed her eyes and sighed. "Mama stop. If it happens it happens. If it doesn't, it doesn't. We're in a good place. You're gonna have to look at Shelly for more grandbabies."

"It's not that," Laura replied. "I just want you to be happy."

"I am happy," Terry said. "Don't have to be married to have that. Besides, look at Bryce. Look at you."

Terry realized her slip too late. Laura slammed her hand on the table.

"What the hell is that supposed to mean?"

Mama cussed, which meant she was really in trouble. Since she was already there, she might as well go all in.

"You and Daddy weren't as slick as y'all thought y'all were," she said. "I heard and saw a lot of things I wasn't supposed to."

Laura's defiant stare withered. She shook her head then took a slice of bread out of the bag.

"I ain't gonna lie to you. Those first few years between me and your daddy were rough. You never really know a person until you live with them. But we worked things out."

"Because you were married?" Terry asked.

"Because we loved each other. Even more, we liked each other. I couldn't imagine my life without your daddy in it, and he felt the same. He's my best friend."

"What about the sacrifices?"

"I ain't never sacrificed anything, and neither did your daddy. A person that loves you will never ask you to give up what's important to you. If they do, that ain't love."

Mama got up, strolled to the refrigerator, and made herself a glass of water.

"Now there's been a whole lot of compromising," she continued. "But that's marriage. I didn't give up anything I miss."

Terry didn't respond. She finished her sandwich.

"João and I started living together two years ago. He's never asked me to change anything. And I haven't asked him."

"Then that man loves you," Laura said.

"He's never said it," Terry replied.

"Does he have to?" Laura asked. "Some people don't tell you. They show you. My parents were hard farm folks. I can't remember either one of them saying 'I love you' to each other or to us. But I knew they did. I knew because of what they did for us."

Laura stood then stretched. "I'm going back to bed. I'll see you later."

She bent over and kissed Terry's forehead.

"Love you, Baby."

"I love you too, Mama."

Terry watched Laura shuffle away before returning to her room. She edged into the bed, then wrapped her arms around João. He groaned.

"Where did you go?" he asked.

"To the kitchen for a snack."

"You should have told me. I would have asked you to bring me back a steak."

Terry giggled then squeezed him tighter.

"I would have," she replied.

João chuckled. "Now go back to sleep."

"João? I love you."
João opened his eyes wide.
"What?"
"I love you."
João smiled. "I love you too, gatinha."
They kissed, her arms reaching under his sleepshirt. She felt his hands slide from her waist then into her pants.
"We'll have to be quiet," she warned.
"You're the loud one," João replied.
"Then keep your mouth on mine."
"No problem at all."
They hurried each other out of their pajamas.

-14-

Shelly's alarm woke her. She threw her sheets aside then shuffled to her closet for her clothes. She put on her jeans and the Christmas sweatshirt she bought when shopping for lights, slid on her house shoes then jogged to the kitchen. She decided the night before she would get up and make everyone breakfast, making sure they were good and full for decorating the tree and the house. This was her first time home for Christmas in a while, and she was determined to make it special.

As she prepared coffee, she thought about Damian. She hadn't spoken to him since he decided to stay in the hotel. As far as she knew, he wasn't mad at her but she hadn't heard from him since. She felt bad about the situation. He'd come all this way to spend Christmas with her, and now he was sitting alone in a hotel room.

"I should text him," she said aloud. "Yeah, I should."

She set up the coffee then took out her phone to text him then changed her mind. She called instead. He answered almost immediately.

"Hey."

"Hey! I'm making breakfast. You want to come over for some?"

"They serve breakfast here at the hotel."

"I'm talking about a real breakfast, not eggs from a carton."

"Ha. Funny. Sure, but I've got no transportation."

"You couldn't get a rental?"

"No. Looks like a lot of people visit Sea Island during the holidays."

"I'll come pick you up."

"I'll walk. The hotel's not far and I could use the exercise. You can meet me at the gate."

"Text me when you get there."

"Cool. And Shelly?"

"Yes?"

"I apologize for this."

"No need to. My family can be a bit much."

"That's not it. We'll talk about it."

"Okay. But after breakfast."

"Okay."

Shelly let the coffee brew while she hurried back to her room to put on a pair of sneakers. When she returned to the kitchen, Bryce was peering into the fridge.

"Hey brother!" she said.

Bryce turned and rubbed his eyes.

"Hey, Lil Sis," he replied. "I wondered who put on the coffee. Thought it was Mama." He eyed her up and down. "And dressed, too? Where you going?"

"Damian's coming over for breakfast."

Bryce nodded. "Good. He shouldn't be here by himself."

"He's catching a ride share to the gate," she said. "I'm meeting him there."

"You want me to?" Bryce asked.

"No. I got it. You can get breakfast started."

Bryce pushed up his housecoat sleeves.

"What we cooking?"

"Everything," Shelly replied. "Grits, eggs, bacon, sausage, pancakes . . . whatever anybody might want. It's almost Christmas!"

"Well, I'll get the grits started," Bryce said. "The rest of that will be waiting for you when you get back. See you in a few."

Shelly rushed out the door and to the SUV. The speed limit for the resort was twenty-five miles an hour, and Shelly pushed right up on it. She was anxious to see Damian, hoping he hadn't lost interest in her. She smiled as she watched him strolling toward the gate wearing jeans, an Air Force sweatshirt, and a jacket. She pulled up next to him and reached over to open the door. Damian climbed in then gave her a sweet, full kiss.

"So, you did miss me," she said.

"How could I not?" he replied.

Shelly grinned. "Maybe you should stay in the hotel the rest of the vacation."

Damian's smile faded.

"About that. I'm sorry for making everything awkward. I caught feelings I wasn't expecting."

Shelly felt a nervous twinge in her stomach, but she was not going to second guess.

"About me?"

Damian kissed her cheek and the feeling in her gut faded. "The only thing I'm sure about is you."

"You don't think we're moving too fast, do you?"

Damian leaned back into his seat. "No. I've been feeling you for a long time. I think we're right where we need to be."

"Well . . . if that's true, you need to share with me," Shelly said. "If something is worrying you, you should tell me."

"I know," Damian said. "It's just that I've been carrying this around for so long, it's hard to talk about."

"Take your time," Shelly said. "I don't plan on going anywhere anytime soon. When you're ready, I'm here."

Shelly pulled into the driveway.

"But right now, it's time to eat. I hope you're hungry because I'm cooking everything."

The house smelled like morning. Bryce had the grits simmering while he sat at the table sipping coffee and scrolling on his phone. Laura was at the stove, watching the bacon and sausage. She turned then shared a smile with them.

"Morning!" she chirped.

"Morning Mama!"

Shelly shuffled to Laura and gave her a hug.

"Good morning, Mrs. Jacobs," Damian said.

"Morning, young man," Laura replied. "Glad to see you here for breakfast. I hope you'll be here the rest of the day."

Damian glanced at Shelly. "I think so."

Shelly and Damian made themselves coffee then sat at the table with Bryce.

"Kids still asleep?" Shelly asked.

"Yes they are!" he said. "I'm happy for the break. They're so excited about Christmas. Took them forever to go to sleep. So, if I nod off during the day, you know why."

"What is Santa Claus bringing them?" Shelly asked.

"Not enough," Bryce said. "Had to cut back because of my situation. But that's okay. Their mother will have more gifts for them when we get back. She'll take any opportunity to make me look bad."

"We're not gonna talk about that," Shelly said. "Good vibes only."

Bryce lifted his coffee cup. "Here, here."

João and Terry strolled into the kitchen.

"Morning, family!" Terry said.

"Bom dia, meu amor!" João replied.

Shelly's eyes shifted between her sister and João. A sly grin split her face.

"Sis, come sit by me," she said.

Terry's eyes narrowed.

"Let me get some coffee first."

João went to stand beside Laura.

"Do you need assistance, Mama Jacobs?"

"From you, of course!" Laura said. "Although we don't have the ingredients you're used to."

"I'll fix that this afternoon," João said. "I'd like to make something special for the family. But this morning, I'll make the eggs."

"Excellent!" Laura said.

"Never let it be said that my man missed an opportunity to show off," Terry commented as she sat beside Shelly. She leaned close to Shelly before speaking.

"I know that tone," she whispered. "What's up?"

"I was about to ask you that, walking in here all glowing and shit."

Terry looked confused. "What are you talking about?"

Shelly sipped her coffee. "Let's just say it's a good thing all these rooms have their own bathroom."

"You are so nasty!" Terry said.

"I'm not the one serving up my man in my mama's house," Shelly said.

Terry chuckled. "First, this ain't Mama's house. Second, it was a mutual serving."

Shelly shook her head. "Lawd."

"And' — she leaned closer — 'I told him I love him."

Shelly squealed. Laura cut her eye at her.

"You alright?"

"I'm fine, Mama, just fine. Terry is, too."

"Be quiet, girl."

Stanley trudged into the kitchen, tying his housecoat belt around his bulging stomach.

"How am I supposed to sleep late with all this noise?"

Shelly jumped from her seat and hurried over to him, Terry close behind. She hugged him, pressing her cheek against his.

"Morning, Daddy!"

Terry mocked Shelly, crushing the opposite cheek with hers.

"Morning, Daddy!"

Stanley laughed.

"Morning, crazy daughters," he said. "Y'all better had left me some coffee."

"I got you, Pop," Bryce said.

"Bryce. The sensible child," Stanley said.

Shelly sucked her teeth. "Anyway, what we got planned for today?"

Bryce looked up. "I don't know. Why don't you tell us?"

Terry laughed. "Yes, Shelly. Why don't you?"

Shelly frowned in mock anger. "I hate both of y'all. Anyway, I thought we would decorate the tree, then we'll drive down to Savannah and hang out for a minute."

"That sounds like a great idea!" João said. "I have a friend that owns a restaurant there. I could get reservations for us."

"You do?" Terry said. "Why didn't you mention this earlier?"

João grinned. "Well, she's not really a friend, but if I contact her, she'll be happy to accommodate us."

Stanley's eyes narrowed. "What kind of food we talking about? Y'all know I don't like all that fancy stuff."

"Trust me, Mr. Jacobs," João said. "You'll love it."

The kids interrupted the conversation. They rushed into the kitchen, climbing Bryce, and kissing his cheeks.

"I'm hungry!" Constance announced.

"Me, too," Cameron chimed in.

"How's that's breakfast coming?" Bryce asked.

Laura looked at João and he winked.

"The eggs are ready!"

"Then let's eat!" Shelly announced.

Laura made the children's plates first, and the adults fell in line. After a quick grace everyone ate. Laura went for João's eggs first. She tasted them then closed her eyes.

"I don't know what you did to these eggs with what's in this kitchen, but you have got to show me!"

João bowed his head. "Thank you!"

"He cheated," Terry said. "Tell her, baby."

"I don't know what you're talking about, Terry," João replied in mock confusion.

Terry took a small seasoning shaker from his pocket and João laughed.

"A special blend of mine. I take it everywhere I go. It helps when I'm confronted with food that needs a little something."

"Like hot sauce in the purse," Shelly said. "You know about that, don't you Mama?"

Laura laughed. "I ain't as bad as your daddy. He took a whole bottle of Uncle Roc's BBQ Sauce to Johnny and Nathan's."

"Daddy!" Shelly exclaimed.

Stanley shrugged his shoulders while he ate. "Their sauce sucks. Ribs are good though. These eggs are good, too."

"You should sell this," Bryce said. "With your celebrity it would fly off the shelves."

"That's the plan one day," João said. "Running a business is hard. I know from experience. Right now, I'm happy with people paying me a lot of money for a little bit of work."

"A man after my own heart," Bryce said. "Big sis, you done good."

"Thank you for your approval, like it mattered," Terry replied.

The kitchen fell silent as breakfast progressed. Tasty food has a habit of doing that. Shelly was first to finish. She took her plate and filled up with seconds.

"Alright now," Terry said. "You're gonna pay for that with pounds."

"I'll just buy bigger clothes," Shelly said. "Besides, I'm on vacation. I'll have plenty of time to get back right with this man's Army PT. Isn't that right, Damian?"

"Yes, ma'am," Damian said, his mouth full of grits.

Stanley took his plate to the sink then began running water.

"Unh Uh," Shelly said. "Sit down. We intruded on y'all holiday, so the least we can do is work."

Stanley grinned. "In that case, somebody get my house shoes."

"Got you," Bryce said. He stood with his plate. "Come on, kiddos. Let's find Granddaddy's house shoes."

"No!" Cameron protested. "They smell like his feet!"

Everyone laughed.

"How do you know that? My feet smell like roses," Stanley said.

"No they don't!" Cameron replied. "They smell like dirt."

"Only one way to find out," Stanley said.

The children took their plates to the sink then followed Bryce down the hall. Damian carried his plate to the sink.

"I'll dry," he said.

"Y'all know we have a dishwasher, right?" Laura said.

"It's okay," Shelly replied. "We got this."

Laura shrugged. "Alright then. I'm going to lay back down."

"You're not going to Savannah with us?" Terry asked.

"I am. Just need a little bit more sleep."

The others piled their plates in the sink then went to their rooms to get ready. Shelly and Damian were alone, working their way through the pile.

"Your family is great," he said. "Y'all love each other so much."

"We do, but we're not always nice," Shelly said. "There's a reason Terry hasn't been home in five years. And Bryce tends to be a little spoiled because he's the only boy."

"Doesn't sound like anything too bad. Terry's here now, and Bryce is a cool brother. I like how he looks out for you and Terry."

Shelly smiled. "He's always done that. Even when we didn't want him to. There were a couple of boys that wouldn't come near me because they heard what Bryce did to the ones that made me cry."

"Damn! It was like that?"

Shelly nodded. "There's a couple of men I should have told him about. But then he'd be in prison."

"Wow. That's love right there."

"Damian, I don't know what it's like to be an only child then have to deal with what you had to deal with. But your daddy is your only family. You should reach out to him."

Shelly braced herself for a harsh reply. Instead, Damian sighed.

"I know, but it's been so long that I don't know how."

"Just call him," Shelly replied. "And I can be there if you need me."

Damian leaned over and kissed her cheek.

"Thank you, Shelly. I'm lucky to have met you. I feel privileged being here with you and your family."

Shelly was speechless. She was familiar with the feelings inside, but she didn't want to act on them, at least not yet. There was pain just below the surface, a storm she never wanted to go through again. Instead, she dried her hands.

"I have to change," she said. "I'll be back."

"I'll be right here," Damian said. "I don't have a choice."

Shelly kissed him lightly on the lips. She turned and hurried to her room, hiding her hopeful smile.

-15-

The family crammed into the SUV and set off for Savannah. Shelly took the wheel, driving the scenic route to the coastal city. The weather decided to cooperate, blessing them with a clear, mild day.

"So where are we going?" Terry asked.

"My friend Julie has a restaurant in Old Savannah," João said. "Do you know where that is?

"I think I do, but I know Google does," Shelly said. "What's the name?"

"Project Parks," João said.

"What?" Bryce laughed. "I hope the food is better than the name."

"It is," João replied. "I guarantee it."

"How do you know?" Shelly asked. "You've never been there."

"All of my friends are excellent chefs," João replied. "They wouldn't be my friends otherwise."

"So, you're a chef snob," Shelly said.

João laughed. "Exactly!"

"I ain't worried," Laura said. "I watch João's show. He's always preparing great recipes. I've made a few of them myself. And I've seen Chef Julie on your show."

"I hope this ain't no fancy food," Stanley said. "I didn't come down here to be bougie. I came down here for some real Gullah cooking."

"It's not, Mr. Jacobs. It's a fresh spin on the local cuisine," João replied.

Stanley huffed. "I've heard that before."

'You'll be fine," Laura said. "If not, we'll take you to Popeye's."

They crossed the bridge into Savannah, parking at the tourist center. The rest of the visit was on foot, strolling the shops of the riverwalk before finding the restaurant. João let the greeter know who they were and a table was immediately set up for them.

They were settling in their seats when Julie Parks emerged from the kitchen, with a wide smile. A halo of curly hair bordered her small, cute umber face, her athletic frame wrapped in a signature apron. Shelly leaned close to Terry.

"So, this is his friend?" she asked.

"Stop it, girl," Terry said. "Being João's girlfriend requires the utmost confidence. The man's a celebrity chef. He knows some talented, beautiful people. That's why I knew he loved me before he said it. The man has choices. As do I."

"Lifestyle of the rich and famous," Shelly joked.

"João!" Julie exclaimed. "You finally made it!"

They hugged and exchanged pecks on their cheeks.

"I wouldn't be here now if it weren't for Terry," João said.

"Terry Jacobs! In my restaurant? Today is a special day!"

Julie hugged Terry and they exchanged kisses.

"It's nice to meet you," Terry said. "This is my family. We're vacationing on Sea Island for the holidays."

Laura and Stanley introduced themselves, and Shelly introduced herself and Damian. The kids made themselves known before Bryce could, and Bryce did his own introductions. Julie's eyes sparkled as she took Bryce's hand.

"What?" he said. "No kiss?"

"No. If I started, I'm not sure I could stop," Julie replied.

"Excuse me," Shelly commented.

"Everyone have a seat," Julie said. "Your server will be right over."

The food was excellent, just as João promised. Julie hovered over them, making sure each meal was perfect. She spent more time talking to Bryce than João, to everyone's amusement. After a few minutes of conversation, they stood to leave.

"I'll get the check," João said.

"I got it," Damian replied.

"No, I insist," João said.

"It's on the house," Julie said. "Good food and good company." She looked directly at Bryce. "I hope you'll come back soon."

Shelly maneuvered between them.

"WE will," she said. "Let's go, everybody!"

They trailed out of the restaurant, sluggish from a satisfying meal. Shelly fell back to walk beside Bryce. She picked up Constance.

"I hope you come back soon," she crooned.

"Stop it," Bryce said.

"Looks like you have an admirer," Terry said.

"The lady knows a good man when she sees one," Bryce said.

"I'm not surprised," Laura said. "My baby boy is handsome."

"And broke," Bryce said.

"Speaking of broke, let's do some shopping," Shelly said. "It's Christmas, and we need some presents under our tree."

"Presents!" Constance cheered.

"Toys!" Cameron shouted.

They walked back to the riverfront shops, halting under the canopy shade of a massive and ancient live oak tree decorated with Spanish moss.

"Now here are the rules," Shelly said. "Everyone buys a gift for everyone else. Nothing expensive unless you're buying something for me. Then the sky's the limit."

Shelly looked at her watch. We'll meet up here in two hours. Okay?"

Everyone nodded their heads.

"Alright, let's do this!"

* * *

Stanley offered Laura his arm and she took it. They strolled around the various shops, perusing the trinkets and other offerings.

"Now this is more like it," Stanley said.

"Yes, it is. And I know just what I'm getting each of the kids."

"Let me guess," Stanley said. "Some kind of seashell for Terry, a novelty item for Bryce, and a Christmas ornament for Shelly."

"Yep," Laura said.

"So, what are you getting for me?" Stanley asked.

"Nothing," Laura replied. "You have me. That's enough."

"True, but I still want a present."

"It won't be a surprise," Laura said.

"It doesn't have to be," Stanley replied. "As long as I have something to open."

"Well, since we're on the subject, I need a present, too."

"I got you one already," Stanley said. "Your present rode down with us from Atlanta."

"No, I want a present from here. Something special to remind me of this vacation. Who knows the next time we'll all be together like this?"

"That's true," Stanley agreed. "Let's get the kids and grandkids something, and then we'll get our presents."

* * *

"Let's go in there."

Terry grabbed João's hand then led him into the small gallery at the end of the cobblestone street. The owner, an older white woman with a kind smile, greeted them.

"Welcome to Sissy's," she said. "I'm Sissy."

Terry shook her hand. "I'm Terry, and this is João."

"Nice to meet you," João said.

Sissy's eyes widened. "I detect an accent. Where y'all from?"

"He's from Brazil," Terry said. "I'm from Atlanta."

"That's what I love about working here," Sissy replied. "I get to meet people from all over the world. There was a couple in here from Lithuania yesterday. But don't let me bore you."

Sissy guided them to the cedarwood wall where the paintings hung.

"All of my paintings are by local artists," she said. "We have some beautiful pieces, and we ship anywhere in the world."

"These are beautiful," Terry said. "Especially this one."

"You have a good eye," Sissy said. "Unfortunately, it's not for sale. Lauren Daniels is one of our best Low Country artists. Her work hangs in galleries throughout the country. She lives nearby on Tybee Island."

"I thought this was a Daniels," Terry said.

"So, you're familiar with her work?"

"Yes. She's one of the artists that inspired me to paint."

Sissy looked curious. "You're an artist?"

"I dabble," Terry replied.

Sissy looked thoughtful for a moment. "What's your last name?"

Terry grinned. "Jacobs."

Sissy's hands flew to her mouth. "You're Terry Jacobs? Oh, my goodness, you're Terry Jacobs!"

Sissy ran to the back of the shop. She returned moments later with a large painting of a tidal creek meandering through the marsh.

"This is you!" Sissy said. "It's just the print, but it's wonderful! I keep it in the back because everyone wants to buy it when they see it and I got tired of saying no."

"May I?" Terry said.

"Of course!"

Terry took the print from Sissy and studied it. "One of my first landscape paintings. So many mistakes."

"It's perfect," João said.

"Can you sign it?" Sissy asked.

Terry studied the print and saw her signature in the bottom right corner.

"It's already signed and numbered," she said.

"I know," Sissy said. "But now I can say you signed it in my shop."

"Only if you'll let me purchase that Daniels painting."

"Done!" Sissy said. She scurried to the back again and returned with an expensive-looking quill pin.

She handed the pen to Terry then took the print from the frame. Terry signed with her usual flourish. Sissy admired the signature as the ink dried, then reframed the print.

"You've made my year!" she said. "Now let's get that Daniels wrapped up for you."

"Can you hold it for us?" Terry asked. "It's a present for my parents and they're with us. We'll come back to get it later."

"Of course!" Sissy said.

Sissy took down the Daniels' painting, replacing it with Terry's print. She went to her desk and returned with her phone.

"Do you mind taking a selfie with me?" Sissy asked.

"Not at all," Terry replied.

Terry and Sissy posed in front of the print and Sissy snapped away.

"Let me take a photo of you two," João said.

Sissy gave him her phone and he took a few more shots. Sissy looked at them and did a twirl.

"The art club members are going to be so jealous!"

Terry paid for the Daniels painting.

"Are you open Christmas Eve?" she asked.

"Yes, until noon."

"We'll be back to pick it up then."

Terry and João left the shop. Sissy followed them to the sidewalk.

"Thank you for stopping by! Have a wonderful time in Savannah!"

"We will," Terry replied.

As they walked away, they heard Sissy's voice.

"Gladys, you won't believe who just came to my store. Terry Jacobs!"

João squeezed her hand. "That was nice of you," he said. "Your parents will love the painting."

"I hope so," Terry replied. "They'll love it more than anything I've done."

"Why would you say that?"

"Because for as long as I've been painting, they have never asked me to do anything for them."

"That doesn't mean they don't like your paintings."

"Then what does it mean?" Terry asked.

"Maybe they don't want to intrude on your time."

Terry felt a chill despite the unusually warm day. She let go of João's hand then hugged herself.

"Never stopped them before," she said.

"Have you ever offered to do a painting for them?"

"I shouldn't have to."

João put his arm around her and the chill subsided. He guided her to a bench shadowed by the broad leaves of a stately magnolia tree. They sat, and he took her hand again.

"Since I was a boy, I wanted to cook. I would watch Mama make our meals, asking her millions of questions as she cooked. Soon she let me add ingredients, stir mixes, and taste seasoning. By the time I was ten, I was her official kitchen helper.

'I was in high school when I decided I wanted to be a chef. I couldn't afford college, so I worked wherever I could, talking my way into some of the finest restaurants in São Paulo. When I finally made it to culinary college, Mama was proud of me. She encouraged me the entire time and was there at my graduation despite her job. But not once would she let me cook for her.

'One day when I was visiting, I woke up extra early and made breakfast. I didn't cook her normal breakfast. I made something completely different. When she came in the kitchen you would have thought I set the place on fire. She fussed at me for not waking her, then she eyed my food suspiciously. I finally talked her into tasting it."

"What happened?" Terry asked.

João laughed. "She took one bite and began crying. 'You hate it,' I said. She shook her head and said, 'No João. This is delicious. Delicious!' Now she never cooks when I'm home."

"So, you're telling me to just give them a painting," Terry said.

"Yes."

"What if they don't like it? I'd be crushed."

"They'll love it because it's from you."

Terry leaned against João. It felt different being close to him. It was better since she told him she loved him. For so long she convinced herself he didn't need to hear her say it, but now she realized it was the final missing piece.

She grabbed his arm then stood, pulling him to his feet.

"Come on. Let's get something to snack on."

"You and the snacks," João said.

"I'm sure somebody here is selling pralines," Terry replied.

"Pralines!?! Where?"

Terry grinned. "You're about to find out."

* * *

"Woah! Slow down!"

Bryce pulled back on Constance and Cameron as they attempted to drag him to the toy store.

"Come on, Daddy!" Constance shouted. "The toy store is right there!"

Shelly and Damian laughed at him.

"So, this is what it's like?" Shelly said.

"Yes, this is exactly what it's like," Bryce replied. "Want one?"

Shelly shook her head. "I'm just fine being Auntie Shelly for now."

She resisted, looking at Damian to see his reaction. Too soon, girlfriend, she thought. She'd made that mistake before and she wasn't going to do it again. Put this one on cruise control and see what develops.

"I can see kids in my future," Damian said. "At least two, maybe three. I love kids, plus it will give me the chance to . . ." Damian fell silent.

"Chance to what?" Bryce asked.

"Nothing," Damian replied.

Shelly studied his face. He had that distant look again, like he was pulling away.

"Let's get in this toy store so I can show y'all what I want," Shelly announced, hoping to break the mood.

"Okay, grown ass woman," Bryce said. "Just make sure you don't run over my kids in the process."

"Ha. Ha."

The toy store was filled with children darting about, followed patiently by their parents and grandparents. Bryce tailed Cameron and Constance as they showed him everything they wanted Santa to bring them. He inspected every toy, making comments about each one. Shelly watched him in admiration.

"He's really good at this," she said to Damian.

"He's been at it for a while," Damian replied.

"I know, but it's just I've never seen him like this. My brother the daddy!"

"I know someone that could learn a few things from him," Damian commented.

Bryce looked at a few more toys then stood up.

"Okay munchkins, time to go!" he announced.

"But you didn't buy anything!" Cameron said.

"No, I didn't," Bryce replied. "Santa is coming in a few days. He'll have plenty of toys for y'all. Trust me."

"But he won't be here," Constance said. "He's gonna leave our toys in Chicago!"

Constance eyes glistened. Bryce squatted and held out his arms. Both children ran to him and he hugged them tightly.

"Santa knows where you are, and I promise you'll get toys here and at home. That is if you've been good."

"We've been good!" they both exclaimed.

"Then you have nothing to worry about," Bryce said.

He stood, lifting them off their feet.

"Now let's go somewhere Daddy can have some fun!"

"Noooo!!!!"

Bryce laughed as he carried the kids outside. He winked at Shelly and Damian. The couple picked up a few of the toys Cameron and Constance said they wanted and threw in a few more to wrap and give to them on Christmas.

"Let's take these back to the SUV," Shelly said.

They were crossing the street on their way to parking when Shelly spotted a familiar face.

"Oh no!" she said.

"What?" Damian asked.

"It's April."

Damian looked at the well-dressed woman walking toward them.

"Yeah, that's her," he said. "I saw her at the hotel. She's quite attractive."

Shelly glared at him. "She broke my brother's heart. She's not allowed to be attractive. Come on, we need to stop her."

"Why?"

"Bryce doesn't want the kids to know she's here. If they see her, they'll want her to come to the house."

Shelly put on a fake smile then strode toward her ex-sister-in-law. "April! What a surprise!"

April looked at Shelly. "Oh. You."

"Nice to see you, too."

April focused on Damian.

"I see you have a new boyfriend. Don't lose this one."

Damian grinned "She won't."

"Sweet," April replied. "Is Bryce here?"

"Yes, he is," Shelly answered. "With the kids."

"Oh my!" April said. "This is not good. I guess I'll leave then."

"That's a good idea," Shelly said. "Best case scenario, you should go back to Chicago."

"Not yet," April replied. "I came all the way down here; I might as well see the sights. Besides, Bryce might change his mind and I want to be nearby when he does."

"Bye, April," Shelly said.

"Goodbye, Shelly. Goodbye, Damian. Nice seeing you again."

April strolled back to her car like a runway model then drove away.

"Let's head back and find everyone," Shelly said. "Time to go. I don't trust that woman."

They hid their packages in the SUV then hurried back to the riverwalk. Shelly texted everyone along the way. They met beneath the big live oak. Everyone pretended to be in a good mood, although it was obvious that Bryce was upset.

"I can't believe she did this," he said.

"It was a coincidence," Laura said.

"She shouldn't be here at all," he continued.

"At least the kids didn't see her," Terry said.

"Let's wait before we go to the SUV," Shelly said. "Me and Damian will go first just in case."

Constance pulled at Bryce's leg.

"What's wrong, Daddy?" she asked. "You look like you do when I break something."

Bryce picked her up then nuzzled her cheek until she giggled.

"Nothing's a matter, little bird," he said.

Shelly and Damian walked back to the parking lot, making sure April's rental car was gone. Shelly texted everyone, and they appeared moments later. After the vehicle was packed and loaded, they drove away.

"Well, I was planning for us to have dinner before leaving," Shelly said. "There's a restaurant that serves great shrimp that I wanted to try."

"Dang," Stanley said. "We haven't had any local fried shrimp since we got here."

"We can always go to Hudleys," Laura said. "Y'all remember Hudleys?"

"Yes we do!" Terry said. She turned to João. "You'd love it. They have their own fishing fleet. Freshest seafood on the island."

"I vote for Hudleys!" João said.

"How about everyone else?" Shelly asked.

"Sounds good to me," Damian said.

"Me, too," Bryce said. "The kids love shrimp."

"Then Hudleys it is!"

A Palmetto Christmas

They left for Hudleys, the overall mood better the further they were away from Savannah. They crossed the bridge to Sea Island forty-five minutes later, following the four-lane highway to the left turn leading to Hudleys. Thankfully, the parking lot wasn't full due to the off season. A young woman with chestnut brown skin, a twist braid crown, and an easy smile greeted them at the door. She led them to a table in the front dining room. Her eyes lingered on João before she left the table.

"Did you see what I saw?" Terry asked.

"I've been recognized," João said.

"Does that mean we'll get another free meal?" Stanley asked.

"I don't know, Mr. Jacobs. We'll see."

"If we keep getting free food when we're with you, I'm gonna let you call me by my first name!"

As if on cue, an older white man sporting a gray beard, flannel shirt and faded jeans entered the dining room from the kitchen. He ambled to the table then placed his large hands on his hips.

"Ladies and gentlemen, we have a celebrity chef in Hudleys," he announced. The other patrons stared at the table as they murmured to each other. The man extended his hand and João shook it.

"Joe Hudley," the man said. "Owner of this little restaurant. I'm a huge fan of your show. I can't believe you're here on Sea Island!"

João slipped his arm around Terry. "You can thank this beautiful woman. We're here on vacation with her family."

Joe grinned at Terry then shook her hand.

"Terry Jacobs," she said. "These are my parents, Laura, and Stanley Jacobs. That's my sister Shelly and her boyfriend Damian. And that's my brother Bryce and his children, Constance, and Cameron."

"Welcome, everybody!" Joe said. He looked at Laura and Stanley. "You two look familiar."

"We should," Laura replied. "We've been eating here almost every year for thirty years. Best fried shrimp in the Low Country."

"You said it, I didn't," Joe joked. "We'll have to put something special together for y'all."

"That's not necessary," João said.

"Speak for yourself," Stanley replied.

Everyone laughed.

"It's our pleasure," Joe replied. He stepped aside and their server came to the table, a dark-haired man with an eager smile.

"Carl will be waiting on y'all," Joe said.

Carl took a slight bow. "Welcome to Hudleys. Is everyone ready to order?"

The family nodded.

"Excellent. I'll take the ladies orders first."

As Carl worked the table, Joe leaned close to João.

"I suggest the shrimp and grits," Joe said. "Best on the island. Hell, best in the Low Country!"

"That's a bold claim," João said. "I'm going to hold you to it."

The meal arrived fifteen minutes later. Joe hovered over the table as the servers brought the plates, paying close attention to João. João scooped up a forkful of shrimp and grits, making sure it contained at least one shrimp. He took a taste then closed his eyes.

"This is excellent," he said.

Joe exhaled. "You've made my day!"

João took out his phone then waved Joe over. Joe knelt beside him and João began recording.

"Hello everyone. Your favorite chef here at Hudleys on Sea Island. I've just tasted the best

A Palmetto Christmas

shrimp and grits in the Low Country according to Joe Hudley, and I believe him."

João turned the phone toward Joe. Joe smiled on cue.

"Y'all come on out for a bowl!" he said.

João shifted the phone back to himself.

"You heard the man. Now let me get back to my meal and my vacation. Tchau!"

João tucked his phone back into his pocket. Joe surprised him with a hug.

"Thank you so much!" he said.

"Good food deserves good exposure," João replied.

Joe stood and patted João's shoulder. "I'll leave y'all to your supper."

"This is good," Shelly said.

"Just as good as I remember it," Terry agreed.

Bryce nodded his head, his mouth full. His phone buzzed.

"Don't answer that," Shelly said. "It might be you know who."

"I have to check," he replied. "Parents rule."

He looked at his screen then smiled.

"It's India."

"Go on then," Shelly said. "You have my permission."

Bryce excused himself from the table then went outside.

"Hey," he said.

"Hey," India replied. "I haven't heard from you, so I thought I'd call."

"I wasn't sure you wanted to hear from me."

"Don't be silly. Of course I did. It's been years and you were my summer boyfriend."

Bryce laughed. "Yes, I was."

"You busy?"

"Having an early dinner with the family at Hudleys."

"I'm sorry!" India said. "We can talk later."

"No, it's cool. What's up?"

"Well, I was wondering if you wanted to hang out. I can understand if you don't have time, but... well, I don't live here anymore, and you're in Chicago, so I don't know when we'll see each other again."

"What are you thinking about?"

"Later today? Can we meet at Folly Beach?"

"Sounds like a plan. Let me see if I can get somebody to watch the kids."

"You can bring them. They'll love our beach."

Our beach. Memories flooded Bryce's mind.

"No. I'd rather it be just you and me."

"I'm glad you said that."

"Let me check. I'll text you."

"Okay. See you soon, hopefully."

"Hopefully."

Bryce went back into the restaurant.

"Daddy, where did you go?" Cameron asked.

"Daddy had a phone call."

"Was it Mommy?" Constance asked.

Bryce frowned. "No, it wasn't Mommy. We'll talk to her tonight."

Constance's face lit up. "Okay!"

Bryce sat and continued eating.

"Well?" Shelly asked.

"She wants to meet later today at Folly Beach."

"Ooooh!"

"Come on, Shelly!"

"What's going on?" Terry asked.

"I'll tell you later," Shelly said. "And we're babysitting."

"Hold up. Don't be volunteering me for work. You don't know what me and João have planned."

"Y'all babysitting with me," Shelly said.

Terry rolled her eyes. "We'll see."

"No need for all that," Laura said. "If Bryce needs somebody to watch the kids, me and your daddy will be happy too."

Stanley looked up from his food with a frown. "I thought this was supposed to be a vacation."

"It is," Laura replied.

"Could have fooled me," Stanley said.

The meal was finished, and Joe served them key lime pie and ice cream on the house. While everyone else indulged, João took a tour of the kitchen and the fishing fleet. By the time he and Joe returned, the family was ready to depart.

Stanley rubbed his stomach. "I think I ate too much. I see a nap coming."

"No, you don't," Laura said. "We need to walk all this off."

"I'll walk it off on my way to bed," Stanley replied.

"A walk would be nice," Shelly said. "What do you think, Damian?"

"I'm game," Damian replied.

They returned to the resort. The kids fell asleep on the way back; Shelly and Bryce carried them to the room and tucked them in.

"For someone who ain't in a hurry for kids, you're sure staying busy with Constance and Cameron," Bryce said.

"I'm the cool auntie," Shelly replied.

"You sure you're good with watching them?"

"Of course. You go get ready."

"Thank you, Sis."

"I just want you to be happy," she said.

"Who said I wasn't?" Bryce asked.

"Come on, don't try it," Shelly said. "Things have been rough, and that woman has always had a way of twisting you up. You didn't even notice Chef Julie at Project Parks flirting with you."

Bryce looked dumbfounded. "She was?"

Shelly shook her head. "My goodness boy. Do you realize that India is trying to restart things between y'all?"

"There's nothing to 'restart'," Bryce said. "We were good friends back then, that's all."

"Damn boy, just go," she said. "We have a house full of family. Somebody will watch the kids."

"Love you, Sis!" Bryce kissed Shelly's cheek and she cringed.

"Yeah, yeah."

Everyone retired to their rooms then returned in beachcombing clothes.

"Somebody has to stay here with the kids," Laura said.

"I will," Stanley replied.

Terry glanced at Daddy. "Me, too."

João gave Terry a curious look. She answered with a nod.

"Okay then," Shelly said. "We'll be back in a few!"

* * *

Shelly, Damian, and Laura exited the back to the boardwalk. Stanley followed them then sat on the back patio. Terry watched him as he settled into the cushioned chair then clasped his hands behind his head. She wasn't sure this was the best time, but there probably wasn't one. She went to the refrigerator and took out two beers. Ambling back to the sliding door, she stopped and took a deep breath.

"Here we go."
She slid the door open then walked to the table.
"You want a beer?" she asked.
Stanley smiled. "Sure do."
Terry opened the beer and put it down near Daddy. She opened hers then sat in the chair next to him. She extended her beer to him.
"Cheers."
Stanley grinned and they tapped the beers together.
"Cheers."
Terry took a swig then waited for it to settle before speaking.
"I'm sorry," she said.
"For what?" Stanley asked.
"For staying away so long."
Stanley shrugged. "No need to apologize. I'm sure you had your reasons. You're here now. That's all that matters."
Terry nodded, trying not to be irritated. It was just like Daddy acting like nothing had happened.
"You don't want to know why I stayed away?"
Stanley stiffened. "Like I said, I'm sure you had your reasons."
"You were the reason," Terry replied.
Stanley sat down his beer. "Me? What did I do to you?"
"You didn't do anything, Daddy. Nothing at all. And that's the point."
Stanley sighed. "Whatever I did, whatever me and your mama did, it was because we thought at the time it was the best thing for you."
"All I wanted to be was an artist," Terry said. "I didn't want to be a 'beauty queen,' I didn't want to be an athlete, a scientist, a doctor, a lawyer, or any of that. I wanted to paint."

"And that's what you're doing," Stanley said.

"But I never got your blessing," Terry replied.

"You just accepted it."

"I didn't stand in your way, did I?"

"You didn't. But you didn't help either. You didn't encourage me. All you would say was, 'That's fine, baby.'"

"I don't see why we're having this conversation," Stanley said. "You're doing what you always wanted to do. You got what you wanted. How I feel about it then or now doesn't matter."

"It does, Daddy. It matters to me," Terry said.

Stanley sat up and turned toward Terry. "Listen," he began. "Me and your mama grew up in different times. You went to school, worked hard, and got a good job. Most of the people we knew that went to college ended up being teachers. We believed the best you could be was a doctor or a lawyer. You're smart, pretty, and tough. We wanted the best for you, and we didn't think being an artist was the best."

"But that's what I wanted!" Terry said.

Stanley sighed. "That's the other thing. Back in the day, we did what we were told. Didn't matter much what we wanted. We expected you to do the same." He extended his hands. Terry hesitated, then placed her hands in his.

"Terry, I'm sorry," he said. "We had high expectations for you. You were doing things me and your mama had never done, soaring higher than we imagined. We wanted for you what other folks told us you should have. We thought we knew what was best. I couldn't imagine you making a living as an artist. That's why I didn't encourage it. Your mama knew better. I hate it when she's right."

Terry laughed and Stanley smiled.

"When I saw your artist career begin to take off, I felt there was nothing to say. You prove us . . . no, you proved me wrong, and I accepted it."

Stanley stood, pulling Terry to her feet.

"I'm proud of you. I always have been, and I always will be."

Terry jumped toward Daddy, hugging his neck tight. Stanley hugged her back.

"I love you, Daddy," she said.

"Love you too, Princess."

Terry pulled away.

"You haven't called me that in years."

"You haven't been around for me to," Stanley replied. "I'm hoping that will change now."

"It will."

They picked up their beers with one hand while still holding hands.

"So, tell me about João."

"He's amazing," Terry said. "Smart, kind, and generous. And I've never met anyone more patient."

"I figure he must be to deal with you," Stanley replied.

Terry laughed. "I'm headstrong, just like you."

"Yes, you are. All of them qualities are nice, but I want to know one thing."

"What's that, Daddy?"

"Is he good to you?"

"Very. And he's good for me. He believes in me and supports me."

"Looks like he's been better to you than me," Stanley said.

"No," Terry replied. "Nobody can be better to me than you and Mama. I wouldn't be who I am if it weren't for y'all."

Stanley took another swig of his beer.

"I know we weren't perfect," he confessed. "We got some things wrong. It was rough for you being the oldest. Bryce and Shelly had it better because we learned with you."

"You sure about Shelly?"

They both laughed.

"Me and your mama were worn out about the time she came," Stanley said. "She got away with a lot more because we were too tired to stop her."

"And she came out alright anyway," Terry said.

"The jury's still out," Stanley replied with a smirk.

Terry finished her beer.

"Want another one?"

Stanley shook his head. "Never thought I'd see the day when I'd be throwing back beers with my daughter."

Terry frowned in mock anger. "You want one or not, Old Man?"

Stanley finished his beer. "Yes, I do!"

They were on their third beer when everyone returned from their walk. Laura was smiling until she saw the bottles on the table.

"Now why you let your daddy drink all them beers? He's gonna be snoring all night and we don't have a spare room for him to sleep."

"You'll just have to tolerate me, bride," he said.

Shelly's eyebrows rose as she counted the bottles. "Did y'all leave any for the rest of us?"

"There's a few left," Terry said.

Shelly went to the refrigerator and brought back the rest of the beer. They all pulled up chairs.

"This is nice," João said. "The ocean has always soothed me."

"This is the most time I've ever spent near the water," Damian replied. "It is nice. Especially in the right company."

"I'm glad y'all came," Laura said. "It's been too long since we've all been together."

"Speaking of all of us, has Bryce come back?" Shelly asked.

"Not yet," Terry replied.

"I hope he's having a good time," Laura said. "He deserves it after all he's been through."

"Here, here," Shelly said, raising her beer. The others did the same.

"I say we get some firewood and put this pit to use," João said.

"An excellent idea!" Terry seconded.

"We can't," Damian said. "Bryce has the SUV."

"We could take the car," João said.

"Bryce is already out. I'll text him," Shelly said. "In the meantime, let's enjoy this wonderful company and the view."

They turned their attention to the undulating waves.

-16-

Bryce steered the SUV into the Folley Beach public parking lot. His heart raced as he backed into the line-faded parking space. He couldn't believe he was so nervous! He felt the same way he did years ago when the family parked in the same lot, hoping he would see India after being away for so long. Except this time he knew he would. And that made him even more apprehensive.

He locked the door then ambled the sandy path leading to the beach. He glanced at the smattering of cars, wondering which one belonged to her. His mind shifted as he walked between sea oats interspersed with palmettos, the hardy shrubs becoming less numerous as he neared the dunes separating the beach from the narrow strip of wetland. As he passed the public washing station he looked to his left. The large driftwood was still there, resting on the edge of the shallow tidal creek separating Folley Beach from the sandy strip further south. India rested on the driftwood, staring out into the gray waves. Almost everything was like it was twenty years ago, except he was now a divorced father of two with no job.

He pushed the thoughts away as he walked toward India, trying his best to block out all the pressure and stress that had accumulated like the broken sea oat stems washed in by the tide. India turned toward him, her caramel eyes meeting his, her infectious smile causing him to mimic her. She stood and walked toward him.

"Punctual as always," she said over the murmuring waves.

"Never one to make a lady wait," Bryce replied.

"One of the things I liked about you."

They hugged and Bryce felt the rest of his tension dissipate. They leaned back from each other, smiling like giddy teenagers on spring break. Then she kissed him, her mouth open, her tongue seeking his. He held her tight, savoring her taste. It was a long, luxurious kiss that ended too soon. India looked dazed.

"Wow. Where did that come from?" she said.

"I'm guessing we missed each other," Bryce replied.

"We never kissed like that before," India said.

"We never kissed at all," Bryce replied.

"We didn't?" India looked confused. "Ever?"

"Never," Bryce confirmed. "You must be thinking about some other summer fling."

"There was only you," India said.

Their fingers intertwined and they walked away from the driftwood. The tidal creek was too deep to cross, and they weren't dressed for it. His mind drifted back again, remembering their long strolls and silly conversations.

"So, I wonder if crabs get cold," India said. "I can imagine them trying to knit little sweaters. One sleeve would have to be bigger than the other to slip over that one big ass claw."

"No skully though," Bryce said. "Not with those flat heads."

"And little crab socks," India added. "Sea Island crab socks."

"We should start a business."

They looked at each other and laughed.

"I'm just realizing right now how much I've missed you," Bryce said.

"Didn't stop you from getting married," India replied.

"That's not fair," Bryce said. "I never thought I'd see you again. And what are you trying to say? That you were holding out for me?"

India made a sad face. "Yes. Yes, I was."

"Liar."

"Give that man a prize!"

India gripped his arm then pressed her head against his shoulder.

"So, how long are you here?"

"Another couple of days," Bryce said. "We'll leave the day after Christmas. I need to get the kids back so they can spend New Year's with April. How about you?"

"Same, but not kids. Going to New York to bring in the New Year. We're gonna freeze our asses off in Times Square."

Bryce peeked behind her.

"That's a lot of freezing."

India swatted his head. "Shut up!"

They fell silent, losing track of time as they wandered the sand, passing other walkers and older couples along the way. Bryce's phone buzzed and he tensed.

"Not again?" he whispered.

"What?" India asked.

"Nothing," Bryce checked his phone. To his relief, it was a text from Shelly.

Get firewood on your way back. We're hanging out at the firepit. And your bad ass kids are awake.

"I got to go," he said.

"So soon?"

"Yeah. I need to make a stop."

They headed back to the parking lot.

"Can I see you again before you leave?" he asked.

"Sure," she replied. "You ever been to the Jazz Cove?"

"No, but I heard about it. That place is hard to get in."

"Not if the owner is your uncle," India said. "I'll make reservations, enough for everyone. The kids can come, too."

"Then it's a date."

They kissed again, less passionate but more sincere. Bryce floated to the SUV, watching India walk to her car and drive away before doing the same. By the time he reached the main road, his mind settled into reality.

"Man, what are you doing?" he said aloud. Nothing made sense. He lived in Chicago; she lived in Charlotte. Things were still complicated with April, and he didn't really know India's situation. Most of all, he was basing all this on a twenty-year-old infatuation. He was smarter than that. Or was he?

His phone buzzed again. He answered without looking.

"I'm on the way," he said.

"I wish you were," April replied.

Her voice threw him off. It wasn't what she said, it was how she said it. She stirred feelings that he hadn't felt for her in a long time, emotions that seemed just under the surface waiting to be released.

"What do you want, April?" he asked. "Are you still here?"

"I'm still here," April replied. "And I want to talk."

"About what?" he asked.

"Us."

A car horn blared. Bryce realized he was still at the stop sign. He pulled into traffic, heading to the convenience store to find firewood.

"What is there to talk about?" Bryce asked. "You told me you didn't want me anymore. You said you had no feelings for me. Hell, you have a boyfriend! What is there to talk about?"

"I can't tell you over the phone," she said. "Something this serious needs to be discussed face-to-face."

"You're afraid I might hang up on you and block your number," Bryce said.

"Yes," April replied. "You have all the reasons in the world to be angry with me. Come by the hotel. It won't take long to say what I have to say."

Bryce squeezed the steering wheel until his fingers hurt. Common sense told him to say no, to hang up and get about his business. But there was that voice inside, that something that formed the first day he saw April in college, that shred of hope that still existed despite everything they'd been through.

"I'll be there in a few," he said.

"Excellent! Thank you, Bryce. You won't regret it. I checked out of the resort hotel. Here's where I'm staying now."

April texted him the address and he punched into his GPS. It only took a few minutes to get there. Once in the parking lot, he texted Shelly.

Had to make a detour. I'll be a little late.
Okay. See you in a few.

Bryce sat in the SUV a few minutes longer, staring at the entrance. He took a deep breath, then got out. The lobby was empty except for the receptionist. The woman smiled at him.

"Checking in?"

"No, meeting a guest," Bryce replied.

"Feel free to have a seat. We have fresh coffee if you'd like a cup."

"I'm fine."

Bryce made his way to the nearest chair and plopped down. Five minutes passed and there was no sign of April. He texted her.

"Where are you?"
"In my room, room 438. Come up."

A shiver coursed his body.

We can meet downstairs.
I told you; this is serious. I'm not sharing our business in public. Come up. Please.

Bryce cursed. He walked back to the desk.

"Excuse me, where are your elevators?"

"Down the hall to your right."

"Thank you."

Bryce trudged to the elevator. Moments later he was on the fourth floor, walking down the wide hallway looking for Room 438. He found the room then knocked.

"Bryce?" April said.

"Yeah," he replied.

He heard the door latch slide aside. April opened the door. She smiled as she held her bathrobe closed with her left hand. Bryce noticed she was wearing her wedding ring. She reached out and grasped his hand, pulling him inside. The room was well appointed, with a comfortable-looking king bed. A wide-screen television was mounted on the wall opposite the bed. Beneath the television was the dresser. A bottle of wine soaked in the ice bucket, a meat and cheese charcuterie board beside it. April sat on the bed; Bryce took the chair at the desk.

"This feels like a set-up," Bryce said.

"Why would I have to set up my husband?" April asked playfully.

"I'm not your husband anymore, remember?"

"That's what I want to talk about," April said. She sat straight, her face suddenly serious.

"I've said a lot of wrong things to you, Bryce. Done some wrong things, too. I'm sorry. I can't explain why, but I know I've hurt you. And through it all, you continued to love me. I think that's why I've done what I've done, because I knew that despite everything you would never stop loving me."

"What are you trying to say, April?"

She looked away; her expression uncertain. When she looked at him again, her eyes glistened.

"I want to know if . . . if you would consider us getting back together."

Bryce sprang to his feet, his emotions in chaos. For years he hoped to hear those words. No, he longed to hear them. Now that she said them, he was confused.

"Get back together?"

April clambered from the bed and rushed at him. Her bathrobe opened, revealing the bra and panties underneath. Bryce's confusion faded away. He grasped her arms and gently pushed her away.

"So, this was a set-up," he said.

April looked confused. "Why do you keep saying that?"

"If you wanted to talk to me, you'd be dressed," Bryce replied. "This was about sex. You figured if that happened, you wouldn't have to say much. And you're probably right. But nothing's gonna happen."

April tied her robe then sat on the bed.

"You sure know how to hurt a woman's feelings."

"See that's just it," Bryce said. "This is about your feelings. It's always about your feelings."

"What are you talking about, Bryce? I love you."

Bryce sat hard in the chair. He was suddenly tired, not physically, but mentally.

"I remember when I first saw you on campus. I'd never seen anyone more beautiful in my life. No, wait. It wasn't just about how you looked. It was your presence. You seemed so confident, so sure of yourself. And then you looked at me as if you saw the same in me. I said to myself that day I was going to marry you."

"And you did," April said. "You were gorgeous. So smart, so focused, so determined."

Bryce chuckled. "But I was never your first choice, not even your second."

"What are you talking about?"

"I'm talking about all the others. The boyfriends that came before me, the ones that deserved more attention than me, the ones that you drifted to in between relationships with me. I was like your landing pad when other men didn't work out."

"It wasn't like that, Bryce."

"It was exactly like that, April," Bryce replied. "But that's on me. I wanted you that bad, so bad that I'd take the crumbs you left for me. You know when I decided to ask you to marry me?"

April looked solemn. "When?"

"When I figured you were done. When you were out of options. I decided you were ready. So, I asked. And honestly, I was surprised you said yes."

"I said yes because I love you. I wanted to spend the rest of my life with you."

Bryce laughed. "Look how that worked out."

"I wish I could tell you why . . ."

"I can," Bryce said. "You got bored. We had it all; good jobs, great house, cute kids, everything. But it wasn't enough. I saw it in your eyes. I'd seen it so many times before. But I thought that since we were married, it would prevent the wandering. But I was wrong. And I don't want to be wrong anymore."

Bryce stood to leave. April grabbed his arm.

"Wait Bryce! You haven't listened to what I have to say. Okay, this was a mistake. I apologize for that. But I still deserve a chance."

"Do you?" Bryce said. "I'm tired, April. I'm tired of trying to make you happy."

"I'll make up to you, you'll see. I promise."

"Let's just focus on the kids, okay?" Bryce said. "Whatever happens after that happens."

He leaned close and kissed her on the cheek.

"Goodbye, April."

"That sounds so final."

Bryce didn't reply. He left the room, closing the door behind him. The elevator ride to the lobby seemed to take forever, as did the walk to the SUV. As he started the engine, he wiped his eyes. He was actually doing it, something he should have done a long time ago. He knew she would always be in his life because of the children, but they would work that out. But he had to move on. He didn't lie when he told her he still loved her. He did. But he deserved a better relationship, one where he was just as important to the person involved as they were to him. He needed love on equal terms, and he would never get that from April, no matter what she said.

 Bryce gave himself a moment, then pulled out of the parking lot. His family was waiting for him, and being with them would help. He merged into the traffic, then set out in search of firewood.

-17-

The family sat around the fire pit, watching the kids cavort on the beach. Laura wrapped her arms around herself then shivered.

"It's getting chilly out here. I'm going in to start dinner."

"What are we having? Terry asked.

"Fried chicken, collards, corn bread, and hopefully red rice."

"Mmm, mmm!" Shelly said. "That's what I'm talking about!"

"You said hopefully about the rice, Mrs. Jacobs," João said. "Is there a problem? Anything I can help you with?"

"No baby," Laura replied. "I called Janine when we got here and ordered red rice and gumbo. Her restaurant is closed at this time of year, but she said she'd make it at home and bring it over. I haven't heard from her in a few days."

"Who's Janine?" Shelly asked.

"Janine Gibson, the lady that owns Gullah Kitchen," Stanley said. "The place with the good redfish."

"Oh, that place!" Shelly said. "I wish it were open. That's good eating. You'd love it, Damian. You too, João."

"Maybe next time," Damian said. His eyes met Shelly's and they both smiled. This was going to last a minute.

The doorbell rang. Terry stood to answer it but Laura waved her down.

A Palmetto Christmas

"I'm heading that way," she said. "João, you want to help me cook? You might learn something."

"Of course, Mrs. Jacobs!" João replied.

João followed Laura into the house. A few minutes later Bryce appeared with two stacks of firewood.

"The man of the hour!" Shelly said.

Bryce smirked. "Brought some kindling, too. I figured nobody had one so I got a lighter."

"The man thinks of everything," Terry said.

"Need some help?" Damian asked.

Bryce shook his head. He paused, looking out to the beach.

"Are those my rug rats?" he said.

"Yep," Terry said. "I'll go get them."

"Let them play," Bryce replied. "I want them to be good and tired when it's dinner time. Exhausted and a full stomach will knock them straight out."

Shelly looked at Bryce sideways.

"You are always trying to find ways to put them babies to sleep. Seems to me you'd be trying to spend more quality time with them."

"Spoken like a person with no children," Bryce replied.

Bryce prepared the pit and Shelly stood beside him.

"How did everything go?" she asked.

"It went great. Much better than I expected. Until April called."

"What!?!"

Bryce lit the kindling. "Yeah. Said she wanted to talk."

"You didn't go over there, did you?"

"I did."

"Dang it, Bryce!"

"She's the mother of my children," Bryce explained. "And I do love her."

"Don't tell me y'all rekindled things," Shelly said.

"We didn't," Bryce replied. "She gave me something to think about."

"I bet she did," Shelly said.

"Not like that. But she tried."

"I never liked her," Shelly confessed. "I never liked how you were around her. Like a puppy dog."

"No you didn't," Bryce said. "She doesn't care much for you, either. But she was my choice and it was good for a long time."

The kindling was burning well, so Bryce added the larger logs.

"No matter what does or does not happen between us, you'll have to respect my choice," Bryce said.

"I did before. I will now," Shelly replied. "But still, I'd rather have India as a sister-in-law. At least she's nice to you."

"Don't get ahead of yourself," Bryce said. "India and I had a good time, but that's about it. I haven't seen her in years. I'm sure she's changed. I have, too."

Shelly waved her hand. "I'm not gonna get in your business."

Bryce burst out laughing.

"You get any deeper in my business I'll need to have surgery to get you out."

The fire increased to a steady blaze. Bryce inspected his handiwork then turned to Shelly.

"Now come help me gather these children."

"Race you," Shelly said.

Bryce took off in a sprint.

"Hey!" Shelly ran after him.

"Y'all gonna hurt y'all selves!" Stanley shouted. "Look at them. Acting like they're nine years old."

"You know how children are," Terry said.

Stanley laughed. "I sure do."

Damian stood up. "Damn, Shelly's fast."

"She is," Stanley said. "Couldn't talk her into running track, though. She played volleyball instead."

"Think I'll join them," Damian said.

Terry and Stanley watched Damian saunter to the beach. Terry looked at Stanley and a sly smile came to her face.

"Want a beer?" she asked.

Stanley grinned. "You read my mind."

* * *

Laura poured canola oil into the non-stick shallow pan then turned on the eye to the gas stove.

"Wish I had my skillet," she said. "We'll make it work, though."

João watched like a focused student.

"What would you like me to do, Mrs. Jacobs?"

"You can get the greens started," Laura said. "I prepared them at home and brought them here. I usually save them for Christmas day, but I guess we can have a taste. You do know how to cook greens, don't you?"

"Of course," João said. "My only question is do you use fatback or turkey."

"Turkey will never see my greens pot," Laura said. "I want my greens to taste good."

João laughed. "Collards with turkey can taste very good with the right balance of seasonings."

Laura put her hands on her hips. "I'm sure that's true, but I don't play with my collards, especially during the holidays. But I'll make you a promise. If you and Terry come by the house, I'll let you cook greens your way."

"I'll take you up on that promise," João said.

João prepped the pot while Laura washed and seasoned the chicken. The doorbell rang.

"Somebody get the door!" Laura called out. "It's probably Janine!"

"I got it!" Terry shouted back.

Laura heard the door open. Terry and Janine exchanged pleasantries then Janine entered the kitchen carrying a Dutch oven filled with red rice.

"Hey, Laura! I'm sorry I'm so late bringing this . . . Oh my goodness!"

Janine almost dropped the rice when she recognized João.

"Laura! Laura! What is João Rebeiro doing in your kitchen!?!"

"Making collard greens," Laura replied.

Janine dropped the Dutch oven on the counter then ran over to João.

"It's so nice to meet you! I watch your show all the time!"

"Thank you," João said. "I appreciate your attention."

"João is here with Terry," Laura said. "He's her boyfriend."

"This is perfect!" Janine said. "Well, it might be."

Laura dropped the chicken breasts into the hot grease.

"Perfect for what?" she asked.

"That's okay," Janine replied. "We'll work it out."

"Work out what?" Laura said.

Janine sat at the table. "Well, every year we make Christmas dinner for the less fortunate at the church on December 23rd. A group of volunteers meet at the church the day before to prepare the meals. But things haven't been the same since the pandemic. We get fewer volunteers, and this year we've hit rock bottom. We won't be able to make half as many meals as the previous year, which means a lot of families won't get a meal this year."

Janine stood. "That's why I was late with your rice. Been cooking since I talked to you."

"Is there something you want to ask, Janine?" Laura said.

"Well, seeing that João is here . . ."

"How can I help?" João asked.

Janine's face brightened. "Well, if the word got out that you would be at the church, I'm sure a lot of people would show up to help."

"Then let's make it happen," João said. "What's the name of your church?"

"Piney Grove Baptist Church," Janine replied.

"Wait just a minute," Laura said. "Janine, I appreciate you going out of your way for us, but João's on vacation. I don't think it's right to ask him to do this."

"I know Laura, and I apologize," Janine replied. "But sister I'm desperate. This dinner means a lot to me, my family, and the community."

"It's okay, Mrs. Jacobs. I'd love to help," João said. "One of the reasons I became a chef was to help others. I think you can spare me for a few hours."

"Spare you for what?"

Terry entered the kitchen in search of more beer.

"Miss Janine has invited me to assist her church members prepare meals for the less fortunate on the 23rd. She feels my presence might increase volunteer turnout."

"Of course, it will," Terry said. "I'd like to help too if you need an extra pair of hands."

"I'm not in the position to turn anyone down," Janine replied.

"What are we doing?"

Shelly, Bryce, and the kids entered the kitchen.

"Miss Janine has invited us to help prepare meals for the underserved at her church the day before Christmas Eve. They're short on volunteers," Terry said.

"That sounds great!" Shelly replied. "A gift to the community."

Bryce looked skeptical. "I'm not sure." He looked at Constance and Cameron.

"They can pitch in too," Janine said. "And we'll have activities when they get bored."

Bryce knelt before the kids.

"What do you say? Y'all want to help us cook?"

"Yes!" they replied.

Bryce looked up with a grin. "We're in!"

"Well alright then," Laura said. "Looks like a change in plans. One of y'all tell your daddy. I'm watching this chicken, and I don't feel like listening to him fuss."

Terry went to the refrigerator and took out two beers.

"I'll tell him."

She and the others left the kitchen. João finished adding seasoning to the greens.

"Tell me Miss Janine, do the local businesses support your efforts?"

Janine sat at the table. "Not really. We've had a few, but not consistently."

"I think I can help you with that, at least with one of them."

Janine's eyes went wide, "Really? That would be amazing."

"I'll make a phone call. Excuse me."

João took out his phone then dialed. He put it on speaker then sat it on the table.

"Hudleys," the voice on the other end announced.

"Hi. This is João Rebeiro."

"Mr. Rebeiro! Yes! How can I help you?"

"Can I speak to Joe?"

"Of course!"

João winked at Janine and Laura while he waited for Joe to come to the phone.

"João!" Joe said. "Good to hear from you so soon!"

"Hi, Joe. First of all, thank you for the meal. It was amazing. The freshness, the seasoning, and the atmosphere were on point!"

"We aim to please," Joe replied. "And your post went viral. We've never been this busy this time of year."

"That's great to hear. Tell me, Joe. Are you familiar with the Christmas charity dinner at Piney Grove AME? They give it every year."

"I'm familiar with it."

"I'm sitting here with Miss Janine, the organizer. She's a family friend. Miss Janine's been having a tough time finding volunteers, so I'm helping out. I was wondering if we could depend on Hudleys assisting as well?"

"We'd be happy to," Joe said. "A favor for a favor. I'll reach out to some of the other restaurants as well. I don't think anyone will say no if you'll be there."

"I will," João said. "Thank you so much. I'm looking forward to hearing from you soon.

"Thank you!" Janine called out.

"Y'all are welcome," Joe replied.

João hung up the phone and shared a wide smile.

"And that's that!"

Janine ran over to him and kissed him on the cheek.

"Thank you so much, João! You're an angel."

"Anything to help."

He checked on the greens, which had come to a boil. He reduced the heat, put the lid on the pot then went to the refrigerator and took out a beer.

"Now if you ladies will excuse me, I'm going to join Terry and Mr. Jacobs by the fire."

"You set a time for those greens?" Laura asked.

"Yes ma'am."

Laura shook her potholder at him.

"Alright now. If those greens ain't right, it's on you."

Laura!" Janine said. "Do you know who you sassing?"

"I do, and I don't care," she replied. "I don't play when it comes to my collards."

João laughed. "I'm on it. I'll be back soon."

João left Laura and Janine alone in the kitchen. Laura took the chicken breast from the pan then added the coated chicken thighs while she spoke.

"I'm glad this worked out for you," she said.

"I apologize," Janine replied. "I really needed the help. Ain't as young as I used to be."

"It's not like we had anything else to do. Now let's get a taste of that rice."

"I'd thought you never ask," Janine said.

She took the lid off the Dutch oven then took a spoon from the drawer. Laura shook her head.

"Not that one. I haven't washed those yet. Get a spoon from the silverware on the counter."

"You know people clean this place before you arrive," Janine replied.

"I don't trust them," Laura said. "They might just run some water on them then dry them off."

"Now you talking about my friends," Janine said. "Some of them clean these rentals."

"Well, when you can let me know which ones they clean, I won't wash them. In the meantime, get that spoon on the counter."

Janine fixed a bowl of rice for Laura and herself. Laura took a taste, smiled, and closed her eyes.

"Oh, my goodness!" she said. "This is better than before! What did you do?"

"I'm not telling," Janine said. "I need your business."

"João!" Laura shouted. "Come taste this rice!"

João entered the kitchen.

"Is this Miss Janine's rice?"

"Yes, it is," Janine said.

João accepted a bowl from Janine and tasted it.

"This is magical!" he said.

Janine slumped into her chair.

"That's it. Lord come get me! The Traveling Chef thinks my rice is magical!"

"It is," he said. "I can't wait to have more."

"How are them greens coming?" Laura asked.

João put down his rice bowl and checked the greens.

"They're coming along fine," he said.

"Well, you sit yourself down in here until they're done."

"João saluted. "Yes ma'am!"

Laura finished the thighs and a few wings for dinner. She lingered in the kitchen, keeping an eye on João and the greens, occasionally speaking to Janine. Dinner was finally done, and she called everyone to the kitchen. Stanley blessed the food and everyone indulged. Laura usually insisted that everyone eat together at the table, but since they were on vacation she didn't complain as everyone found their place to enjoy. Laura and Janine remained in the kitchen; João went back to the firepit with Terry and Stanley.

Laura took a forkful of greens. She took a taste and her eyes went wide.

"What's wrong?" Janine said.

Laura raised her hand as she shook her head. She chewed as she hurried out to the patio then stood before João as she swallowed, João looking at her with a smirk on his face.

"Uh oh," Stanley said. "I think you're in trouble." Terry nodded in agreement.

Laura took one last swallow.

"João Rebeiro, what did you do to my collard greens?"

"I may have added a few things while you weren't looking," he confessed.

Terry tasted her greens. "Why are you complaining, Mama? They taste great."

"I know," Laura said. "They taste better than mine."

"So why you upset, baby?" Stanley asked.

"Because I don't like people tampering with my greens," Laura said. "Now they're gonna have to taste like this every time. And I don't have any of that chef's secret stuff, Mr. Rebeiro!"

They both laughed.

"I'll share it with you after dinner," João said. "But it will be our secret."

They finished the meal. Stanley finally left the firepit, going inside to watch television. Shelly and Damian remained outside, listening to the ocean waves. Terry and João retired to their room for the night. Bryce took the children inside and got them ready for bed. He joined Stanley and Laura in the family room, his attention bouncing between the kids and the screen. His phone buzzed and he hesitated. He wasn't in the mood to talk to April. He considered not answering, but he looked and the screen. It was India.

"Hey."

"Hey Bryce. So, are y'all busy tomorrow night?"

"Not that I know of. What's up?"

"I made the reservations for the Jazz Spot."

"Cool! I'll let everyone know."

"Great! I'll see you tomorrow!"

Bryce hung up and put the phone back in his pocket.

"Who was that?" Stanley asked.

"India. She got us a reservation at the Jazz Spot. Want to go?"

"Yes, we do!" Stanley said. "You know how hard it is to get in that place?"

"Her uncle owns it," Bryce said.

"You sure you want us along?" Laura asked.

"It's not like that," Bryce replied. "She got reservations for all of us. Even the kids."

"Well, we can't turn that down," Laura said. "I guess we'll be at the Jazz Spot! I wonder who's playing?"

"Doesn't matter. We're going to the Jazz Spot. Whoever is playing, we'll enjoy it," Stanley replied.

"I'll let everyone else know."

Bryce made the rounds. Terry answered the door to the bedroom, looking a bit flushed. Bryce smirked then went to the patio to let Shelly and Damian know. They looked at each other before Shelly answered.

"We'll think about it," Shelly said.

"Y'all don't like jazz?" he asked.

"We do, but it will be kind of nice to have the house to ourselves for a while."
"Cool. Let me know when y'all decide."
"We will."
The night lingered on. One by one they retired to their rooms, the kids first, Laura and Stanley, and then Shelly. Bryce and Damian sat alone in the family room, channel surfing. Damian stood and stretched.
"I think I'm gonna go back on the patio," he said.
"Care for some company?" Bryce asked.
"Sure," Damian replied.
"Want another beer?"
Damian smiled. "I can use one."
Damian headed to the patio while Bryce went to the kitchen for beer. Damian was throwing a few more logs on the fire when he arrived.
"Here you go."
"Appreciate it."
They sat and opened their beers. Damian took a swig then gazed out where the ocean was barely visible with the firelight. Bryce drank then looked at Damian.
"So how did you meet Shelly?" he asked.
"My roommate was dating her friend," Damian replied. "She thought we would get along, so they invited us to dinner with them."
"And they were right," Bryce said.
Damian nodded his head. "I'm not an outgoing person. I like to keep to myself, play video games, that sort of stuff. But Shelly is just the opposite."
Bryce laughed. "That's an understatement. The girl will talk to a tree for an hour before she notices it's not talking back."
Damian laughed. "She's friendly, but not in an annoying way. It helps that she's beautiful."

"Beautiful? I guess so," Bryce said.
"Brothers," Damian replied.
Bryce finished his beer. "So y'all must be pretty serious if she asked you to come home with her."
"That's just it," Damian replied. "I didn't know we were until she asked."
Bryce's face took on a concerned look.
"What do you mean by that?"
"Don't get me wrong," Damian replied. "I wanted us to be closer. But Shelly seemed to be holding back. I was happy when she asked."
"You say serious," Bryce asked. "How serious?"
Damian smirked. "When I came to sit out here, I didn't realize I was gonna get the third degree."
"That's fair," Bryce replied. "But I'm always looking out for my sisters, especially Shelly. She just got out of a bad relationship, and I don't want to see her hurt again."
Damian sat his beer down.
"Look Bryce, I can't say I understand how you feel. I'm an only child, except for my stepfamily, and for reasons they don't count. I can't tell you how things are gonna work out for me and Shelly. Right now, it's good. Real good. It's not in my plans to hurt her. I don't think anybody plans that. But she was ready to take a chance with me. Maybe you should be, too."
Bryce grinned. "I like a brother who's straight up. And you're right. I should trust Shelly."
Bryce raised his bottle and took a drink.
"You're a cool dude, Damian. I think you and Shelly will be together for a while."
"I hope so," Damian replied.
"That still doesn't mean I won't beat you up if you hurt her," Bryce said. "It's my brotherly duty."
"I'll keep that in mind," Damian said.

Bryce finished his beer then stood.

"I'll let you have your quiet time. Good night."

"Good night, Bryce."

Damian watched Bryce go back into the house then shook his head and smirked. He turned his attention back to the dark void before him, listening to the waves pulsing against the sand. A few minutes later, he was asleep.

-18-

The family slept late, waking up almost at nine. Shelly was the first to rise as always, then flittered about waking everyone else.

"Get up y'all! We're late!"

She knocked on everyone's door then hurried to the kitchen.

Stanley sat up and rubbed his eyes. "Late for what?"

Laura rolled over to look at the alarm clock.

"Janine's dinner preparation," she said.

Stanley fell back onto the bed.

"Y'all can go without me," he said. "I think I drank too many beers last night."

"This is the best way to sober you up," Laura replied.

She groaned as she got out of bed then shuffled over to Stanley.

"Come on, handsome. Let's get washed up."

Laura pulled at his arm and he stood.

"Some vacation this is turning out to be," he complained.

"You know you're enjoying it. Now come on."

Bryce trudged into the kitchen.

"What's for breakfast?" he asked.

"Sausage biscuits," Shelly chirped. She'd thrown on her new Sea Island sweatshirt and jeans.

"I'm going to McDonalds to pick them up. You can text me if anybody wants anything else."

"I refuse to eat that."

João walked into the kitchen, Terry beside him.

"Then make something quick," Shelly said. "I'll be back in a few."

"Bring back maple syrup," Terry said. "The real kind, not that fructose crap."

Shelly waved her hand over her head as she walked out the door.

"Help me," João said to Terry.

"What are you cooking?" Terry asked.

"French toast," João answered.

The toast was done by the time Shelly returned with the sausage biscuits and maple syrup. After a satisfying breakfast, they loaded into the SUV and headed for the church. The parking lot was full when they arrived.

"Good turnout!" Shelly said.

"We know why," Damian replied. He and João did a fist pump.

"I love using my powers for good," João said.

"Let's get inside before Janine thinks we stood her up," Laura said.

They hurried to the rear of the church, greeting the volunteers along the way. When they entered the kitchen, all heads turned. Janine stood at the opposite end near the ovens. The worried look on her face transformed into a relieved smile.

"They're here!" she said.

João took the lead. The crowd recognized him and broke out in applause. He grasped Terry's hand and led her up front with him.

"Sorry we're late," he said to Janine. "We had a late night."

"As long as you're here baby," Janine replied.

"May I?" he asked.

Janine stepped aside. "Please do."

João stepped forward, sharing his warm smile with everyone.

"What a crowd! You would think you were expecting someone special!"

Everyone laughed.

A Palmetto Christmas

"Thank you all for coming," he continued. "When Miss Janine told us about this amazing dinner, we knew we had to participate. Growing up in the favelas of São Paulo, I know firsthand what it means to be poor, and I also know how just a little help will go a long way. I'm happy to see so many people volunteering to brighten someone's holiday. It's the reason for the season."

João could see the embarrassed smiles on some of the volunteers' faces, the ones that would not have come if not for him. He wasn't about to give them a pass.

"Now I know there are a few of you who volunteered because you heard I would be here. It doesn't matter. You're here and we're thankful for it. But I hope this won't be just a one-time thing for you. I hope you'll be infected by this spirit and you make it a Christmas tradition. Now I'm going to turn things back over to Miss Janine, and she'll give us our marching orders."

João gave the floor back to Janine.

"Thank you, João," Janine said. "Seeing all y'all here brings tears to my eyes. But we're not here to ogle, we're here to work. Can I ask my veteran helpers to come forward?"

The church members joined Janine, smiling and greeting everyone along the way. They wore jeans and matching sweatshirts that read 'Piney Grove Loves You.'

"These lovely people will give everyone their assignments," Janine said. "Our goal is to make enough food to serve twelve hundred dinners tomorrow. With the people we have here today, I think we can do it and then some. Let's get it started!"

And with those words, the cooking began. One of the younger members took out a portable speaker and sat it on one of the tables. Moments later Donny Hathaway's melodic voice filled the room as he sang 'This Christmas.' Laura and Stanley sang along with most of the volunteers, and Shelly, Bryce, and Terry joined in.

Janine's helpers were kind and professional, handing out assignments equally with no preference. Terry was on duty opening cans, while João labored with Miss Janine cleaning and prepping turkeys. Laura and Stanley were on cornbread. Even the children had duties, making sure the grownups had plenty of beverages. When lunchtime came, one of the restauranteurs scheduled a fleet of food trucks that offered everything from tacos to beef patties.

Shelly and Damian received instructions on the proper way to clean and cut collards from Miss Betty Jenkins, a small woman with bright eyes and large hands. After working through a few bunches, they were left on their own with the others.

"I apologize for this," Shelly said to Damian. "I know you didn't come all the way from Germany to work."

"Don't apologize," he replied. "I volunteered, remember? Besides, this is great. I love the energy, and I love being here with you."

Shelly shoved him with her elbow.

"I'm glad you're here too," she said.

They focused on their duties for a few minutes, Shelly stealing glances at Damian as he cleaned and cut. A warm feeling rose inside of her, the one that let her know she'd fallen. It was too late now. She liked him; she liked him a lot.

"Damian," she said. He looked at her and smiled.

"What?"

"How do you feel about us?" she asked.

Damian grinned. "I feel just fine."

Shelly took a breath. "Okay, I know this probably isn't the time, but do you see us together for a long time?"

"I do," Damian replied. "For as long as you'll have me."

Shelly dropped her head to hide her wide grin.

A PALMETTO CHRISTMAS

"You know, I had a conversation with Bryce last night," he said.

Shelly looked up suddenly. "Oh no! What did he say?"

Damian laughed. "He asked me what were my intentions with you."

"That man is not my daddy," Shelly replied.

"He's just looking out for you," Damian said. "I can understand that. He loves you and he doesn't want to see you hurt again."

"And what did you tell him?"

"I told him I had no intention of doing that."

Shelly nodded. "Did he threaten to beat you up if you did?"

"Yes. Although I think I can take him."

Shelly pushed him playfully. "Let's hope it doesn't come to that."

Damian's expression became sincere. "It won't."

With so many volunteers the day passed quickly. By early afternoon, the food had been cooked and meals prepared. The holiday spirit permeated the room, with smiles, and laughter in abundance. Janine grabbed an empty pot, hitting it with a metal spoon to get everyone's attention.

"Well, it looks like we're done!" she announced.

The room exploded in applause.

"Thank y'all so much for coming! We did it again. Not only did we meet our meal goal, we surpassed it! That means we'll be able to serve more people than ever."

Janine shared a smile with the Jacobs.

"Thank you, João, and the Jacobs for your support. We wouldn't have had this kind of turnout if not for you."

"You're welcome!" João said. "And I'd like to let you and everyone know that this will be an annual event for me. See you next year!"

Janine covered her mouth as she cried. Everyone stopped to shake João's hand as they left the cafeteria. Joe Hudley gave him a hug.

"You're a good man, João. It took someone from out of town to get us to support our own. I must admit I'm a bit ashamed that we haven't been involved before. Some of the people receiving dinners tomorrow work for me. We're going to have to do better."

"I appreciate you coming and bringing everyone with you," João said.

They shook hands and Joe left with the others.

"Let's head back to the house and rest," Bryce announced. "We have a date tonight!"

* * *

The family prepared for the evening festivities. Laura and Stanley retired to their room and napped, as did Bryce and the children. Terry and João lounged in the family room, listening to their jazz playlist and small talking. Shelly was heading for the patio when Damian touched her shoulder.

"Walk with me," he asked.

"Okay."

Shelly took his hand and they headed for the beach. They strolled in silence for a while before Damian spoke.

"I think I'm going to call my dad," he said.

"Really? That's great!" Shelly replied.

"Is it, though? We haven't spoken in years, and to be honest I'm still angry. But being around your family and seeing how y'all get along makes me want to try."

"I think you should," Shelly said. "I know it's been rough, but he's your daddy."

Damian frowned. "If that's so, why hasn't he tried to contact me? That's what makes me hesitate. I'm the child."

"You're not a child anymore," Shelly said. "One of the most significant things that happened to me was when I realized my parents were human. That they had flaws and made mistakes just like me."

"I never thought he was perfect," Damian said.

"Somebody has to be the hero of this relationship," Shelly said. "It might as well be you. And if it doesn't work out, at least you tried."

"Will you be there when I call him?" Damian asked.

"Of course I will," Shelly replied.

Damian let out a sigh. "Good. I don't think I can go through with it without you."

"Oh, so I'm your emotional anchor now?"

"Yes," Damian replied.

Shelly felt a bit nervous and yet pleased. They were on the same page. This would not be like before.

"When do you want to call him?" she asked. "Now?"

"No, no!" Damian said. "I need time to prepare. Let's just walk. I need a little space after this morning."

"I didn't take you as an introvert," Shelly said. "You seem to be comfortable whenever we met at the club."

"That was because of you," Damian replied. "I'm usually fine in my room with my games. Roomie practically forced me to come that night. I'm glad he did."

"I'm glad he did, too."

Shelly stopped walking, a look of concern on her face.

"What?" Damian asked.

"I'm not gonna be one of those frustrated girlfriends trying to get my man off them video games, am I?"

"You won't be," Damian said. "I can miss a game. I can't miss you."

They stopped for a long kiss.

"Now that we've got that settled, let's get back," Shelly said. "I need to decide what I'm wearing tonight."

"So we're going?"

"Yes."

Damian put his arm on her shoulders while she hugged his waist.

"Whatever you wear, you'll look good in it."

Shelly glowed. "Of course I will."

* * *

"Zip this up for me."

Stanley put on his sports coat then ambled to Laura to zip up her dress.

"I'm glad we packed some dress clothes," she said. "I wasn't expecting to go anywhere, but you never know."

"You look good, baby," Stanley said. "Smell good, too."

"Thanks, handsome," Laura said. "It's been too long since we've gone out. We used to never miss a party or a concert. What happened to us?"

"We got old and boring," Stanley said. "Just like our friends."

"Well, things are going to change once we get back home. I got too many good dresses to only wear to church."

Stanley inspected his head as he brushed his hair then frowned.

"I need to go ahead and shave my head."

"No, you don't," Laura said.

"I don't bother you about your hair, so don't bother me about mine."

"That's different," she said. "You never criticize a woman's beauty choices. Men, on the other hand, need constructive criticism. We need to make sure y'all look as good as us when we go out."

Laura walked over to Stanley. She picked up his hairbrush and brushed his hair.

"You look good. Let's go."

Shelly and Damian were waiting in the family room. Bryce walked in moments later with the children, followed by João and Terry.

"Everybody looks so good!" Shelly said. "Bryce, I can't believe you did Constance's hair by yourself!"

"Comes with the job," Bryce said.

"And Cameron looks like a little man!" Terry said.

Cameron grinned then hid behind Bryce's leg.

"Let's go," Bryce said. "Reservations are at 6:00 pm. We have ten minutes."

"Good thing it's a small island," Stanley replied.

The drive to the shopping plaza took five minutes. Bryce saw India standing in front of the club as they pulled up. She wore a simple black mini-dress with a pearl necklace that accentuated her regal neckline. Her braids rose in a bundle over her head, a few falling loose and bordering her cheeks.

"Wow," he said.

"Wow, indeed," João seconded.

"Watch it, buster," Terry said in mock anger.

Shelly was the first person out of the car. She tiptoed to India and hugged her.

"Hey, girl!" she said.

"Hey Shelly!" India replied. "You haven't aged a bit."

"I hope I have," Shelly said. "The last time I saw you, I was ten."

Laura and Stanley walked up to India and hugged her as well.

"I can't believe this is the little girl that used to be distracting our boy on vacation," Laura said.

India flashed an embarrassed smile. "Hey, Mr. and Mrs. Jacobs. It's so good to see you."

Bryce and the children were the last to approach her.

"Here they are," Bryce said. "Constance and Cameron."

India knelt in front of the kids.

"Hi there!"

"Hi!" the children said together. They lunged to hug her, almost knocking her over.

"Wow. They're friendly," she said.

"Okay, let Miss India loose," Bryce said. The children came back to Bryce and took his hands.

"You look amazing," he said.

"You do too. Let's go inside. The show is about to start."

They followed India into the club. The Jazz Spot was cozy, with booths along the walls and a few tables in the center. A small stage was opposite the entrance, just large enough for a quartet. The tables closest to the stage were empty.

"That's us?" Shelly asked.

"Yes," India answered. "A special place for special people."

A server appeared soon after they sat and took everyone's drink order. India sat near Bryce, Cameron sitting between them.

"I see you weren't lying," Bryce said.

"What made you think I was?" India asked.

"You know how people say they have the hookup and then don't."

"Have you ever done that?" India asked.

"I plead the fifth," Bryce replied.

India laughed. "I never lie about contacts. As a matter of fact, here comes my uncle now."

Bryce turned to see a tall, heavy-set man with chestnut brown skin and a short, gray afro that matched his thick beard and mustache. He greeted the patrons as he made his way to their tables. The man smiled, exposing a gold tooth among his perfectly pearly teeth.

"India! I see your friends have arrived," he bellowed.

India stood and hugged him. "Thank you for this, Uncle Charles."

"Don't mention it. Anything for my favorite niece."

"Your only niece," India said.

"Same difference," Charles replied. He turned his attention to the table.

"Thank y'all for coming," he said. "Allow me to formally introduce myself. I'm Charles Mingus, owner of this fine establishment. Everybody calls me Charley except my niece. She's bougie like that."

Everyone laughed as India glared at him in mock anger.

Charley scanned the table, his eyes lingering on João. "I hope y'all enjoy tonight's set. The band is gonna play a little bit of everything. Might even play some original music. We have a great menu, so feel free to indulge. It's on the house."

"You don't have to do that," Laura said. Stanley gave her a cross look.

"It's my pleasure," Charley replied. "Any friends of India are friends of mine."

Charley looked at his watch.

"Time to get started. Y'all enjoy."

Charley climbed onto the stage and sat before the piano.

"So, your uncle plays the keys!" João said.

"Yes, he does. Julliard trained. He toured the world with his trio until he decided to retire. Came back to the island and opened the Jazz Spot. That was twenty years ago."

"I played around with music for a while," João said. "Thought it would be my way out of the favelas. God had other intentions."

The other band members arrived and the quartet took a minute to warm up as the patrons were served. Charley stood from the piano and took center stage.

"Hey y'all, welcome to the Jazz Spot!"

The audience applauded.

"Thank y'all for continuing to come out for all these years. It's Saturday, so we play what we feel. We'll drop a few familiar songs, and maybe a few original tunes as well. For those of you who come every weekend, you know who we are. For our new folks, I'll make the rounds."

Charley stepped back to the band.

"On bass, we got Bryant Sheppard. On drums, Kiki Green, and on trumpet, Julio Sanchez. You know who I am."

The crowd laughs.

"Let's do this," Charley said.

The band started with a lively swing tune that had hands patting on tables and feet tapping on the wooden floor. João stood and applauded after Charley's solo.

"Bravo! Bravo!" he shouted.

"Okay then," Shelly commented.

"João really loves music, especially jazz," Terry said.

"Okay. I just hope he doesn't embarrass us."

"It's possible," Terry replied. "But I'm used to it."

The children wriggled in their seats to the song.

"Future jazz fans I see," India said.

"They like all kinds of music like their daddy," Bryce replied.

"Didn't know you were a jazz head."

"We didn't spend that kind of time together."

"Maybe we will."

A Palmetto Christmas

Bryce smiled, but he didn't answer. The kids, April, the distance . . . it was hard for him to see it working, as much as he wanted to try.

"I miss this so much," Laura said. "When we get back home, we need to find a good jazz club near us."

"Yes, we do," Stanley replied. "We're old but we ain't dead."

"I know that's right!" Laura said.

They raised their glasses and toasted.

The band played three more songs before taking a break. Charley winked at their table before leaving the stage, giving João another long look.

"He really seems interested in you," Terry said.

"Comes with the territory," João replied. "If he keeps playing the piano like that, he can sit on my lap."

Terry laughed. "No, he can't. That's my spot."

Their server came to the table.

"Would anyone like dessert?"

All eyes fell on India.

"They would," she said. "When my uncle says it's on the house, it's on the house."

"Well, in that case, I'll have a slice of your key lime pie," Laura said.

"It's the best on the island," the server replied.

"Don't tease me, baby," Laura said. "I'm serious about my key lime pie."

Everyone else placed their orders. The quartet returned to the stage a few minutes later, Charley taking the mic.

"I hope y'all enjoyed the first set," he said.

The audience clapped.

"I want to take a minute to thank the Jacobs family for sharing their Christmas vacation with us." The family turned and waved.

"I also want to acknowledge a celebrity in the house, João Ribeiro the Traveling Chef!" Charley continued.

João shook his head and chuckled before rising from his seat and waving.

"Now I don't usually do this, but I have a good reason. I happen to know that Mr. Ribeiro is not only an amazing chef, but he's a decent jazz singer, too."

João's eyes went wide. "How did you find out?"

Charley grinned. "There's this thing called the internet. There are no secrets to it. Why don't you come up and join us for a song?"

"No, no," João replied.

Terry leaned toward him. "Go ahead. You know you want to."

"I'm trying to keep a low profile."

Shelly laughed. "Could have fooled us."

The audience began clapping and whistling. João stood, looking at them then back to Charley.

"Okay. One song," he said.

The audience cheered and Charley waved him up.

"Do you know . . ." João whispered into Charley's ear.

"Sweet," Charley said. He went to the other band members, sharing João's request then sat at the piano.

"Y'all gonna like this one," he said. "It's for the lovers."

Charley played an enchanting solo intro, João listening with eyes closed. He raised his head slowly then looked into Terry's eyes. He sang in Portuguese, his soft, lilting voice carrying throughout the small space. Terry was entranced. Though the song wasn't a love song, it was the emotion in João's voice that captured her. She felt each word in her heart. The rest of the band joined in, filling the club with a smooth bossa nova vibe.

Shelly leaned close to her.

"Girl, I'm glad he told you he loves you. Cause I think I'm falling in love with him right now."

Shelly's words broke the trance. Terry giggled.

A Palmetto Christmas

"You and probably every woman in the room." She looked at the others at the table. Laura and Stanley held hands, swaying to the bossa nova rhythm. Bryce draped his arms around the children, but his eyes were on India, and hers on him.

The song ended as softly as it began. The audience came to its feet, clapping eagerly. João sat beside Terry; before he could say a word, she kissed him.

"You never sang to me before," she said.

"You never told me you love me before," João replied.

"So, it gets better?" she asked.

"Melhor ainda," he replied.

The show ended at 9:00 pm. The children were dozing off, so Bryce and India carried them to the SUV then secured them in their car seats.

"Thank you so much India," Laura said. "This was a treat."

"You're welcome, Mrs. Jacobs. I'm glad y'all had a good time."

Everyone hugged India before climbing into the SUV. Bryce waited until the others were inside before giving his hug.

"Thanks, India. For everything."

"You're welcome. Hey, what are you doing tomorrow?"

"Tomorrow's Christmas Eve, remember?"

"Oh, that's right! Mama's probably going to have something for me to do."

Bryce looked thoughtful. "I was planning on taking the kids to Harbor Cove. They're gonna be excited, so I need to give them a full-day workout to get them to sleep. Otherwise, I'll be up until 3:00 am waiting for St. Nick."

"What time do you plan on getting there?"

"Afternoon, probably one," he said.

197

"Well, if I have time I'll come through."
"That would be very nice."
India began to kiss him but stopped.
"The kids," she said.
"Yeah," Bryce replied. He hugged her again.
"See you tomorrow, hopefully," he said.
"Bye."
Bryce got in the SUV and they were on their way.
"That was really nice," Laura said.
"It was," Terry replied.
"It's been a long time since we did something together as a family," Stanley said.
"We need to do it more often," Shelly replied.
"Y'all children out there living your own lives now," Laura said. "That's the way of things. Don't feel bad about doing what you're supposed to do. But don't forget about me and your daddy. It's good to see y'all every now and then."
"Yes ma'am," Bryce said.
"Gotcha," Shelly replied.
Terry nodded her head.
Once they reached the house Shelly and Terry carried the kids in and put them to bed. Everyone retired to their rooms except Bryce. He went out to the patio, built a fire then sat. He closed his eyes, listening to the ocean.
"Quite a night, wasn't it?"
Terry loomed over him, two beers in her hand. Bryce grinned and took one. Terry sat beside him.
"It was," he said.
"So what are you gonna do?" she asked.
"About what?"
"Come on, brother. About India. That woman is sweet on you like sugar in sweet potato pie. And it's obvious you're feeling her, too."

"I don't know," Bryce replied. "I'm trying to treat it like our summer flings, but this is beginning to stick. It's the last thing I need right now."

"You talking about the kids?"

"The kids and April."

Terry rolled her eyes. "Damn, you really love that woman. After all she's put you through."

"The heart wants what it wants," Bryce said. "But I have to admit things feel different this time."

Bryce sipped his beer. "A year ago, if I had gone up to that room it would have been over. We'd be back together. But now? I surprised myself when I walked out."

"Maybe it's because now you know you have options," Terry said.

"I can't do it because of that," Bryce replied. "I have no idea what's going to happen between me and India. But I can't say April and I are truly over because of her. I don't want to go from one relationship to another."

"I understand," Terry said. "João and I relationship has changed since we've been here. It's always been stable, but it's jumped to the next level. I didn't even know there was another level."

Bryce gave Terry a side-eye. "Is my big sister opening up to somebody?"

"I think so," Terry replied. "I feel like Shelly."

"Hey, don't use my name in vain."

Shelly strolled onto the patio wrapped in her housecoat then plopped down in a chair.

"Aren't you cold in that?" Terry asked.

"I'm warm enough," Shelly replied. "So why y'all talking about me behind my back?"

"It wouldn't be the first time," Bryce said.

Shelly punched his shoulder. "For real, though. What y'all talking about?"

"Changes," Terry replied.

"I know that's right," Shelly said. "There's been a lot on this trip. Mama and Daddy holding hands like teenagers, Bryce and India with them smoldering eyes, and you Terry? I thought you were gonna tackle João on that stage!"

They laughed.

"What about you and Damian?" Bryce said.

Shelly became serious. "We're both trying to pump the brakes on this thing."

"Why?" Terry asked. "You've always been one to fall fast, and now you're with somebody that wants the same."

"I know, and it's great," Shelly said. "But still . . ."

"I say let it ride," Bryce replied. "Don't let the pain of a previous relationship stop you from loving again. Ain't no guarantees with this love thing. Got to take it day by day."

"That's true," Terry said.

They sat silent for a moment, each in their own thoughts.

"I like this," Shelly said.

"What?" Bryce asked.

"Sitting here with y'all. Not doing anything in particular, just existing."

"We should plan to get together every year," Terry said.

Shelly and Bryce looked shocked.

"You want to get with us every year?" Bryce said. "Damn, this has been some trip!"

"Very funny," Terry replied. "I haven't been avoiding y'all. Mama and Daddy, maybe. But you two? No. As much as y'all used to get on my nerves when we were little, I love you. Life gets so busy sometimes you don't know what you're missing until it's in your face."

"It's worth a try," Shelly said. "I never know where this man's army is going to send me, but we can work it out."

"Everything for me is up in the air right now," Bryce said. "I have no idea where I'm going to be working, let alone where I'm going to be living."

"We don't have to plan it now. Let's just make sure we don't forget," Terry said.

"It's a go then," Shelly replied. "And for the record, it wasn't me getting on your nerves. That was Bryce one hundred percent. I was too cute and adorable to get on anybody's nerves."

"Girl please," Bryce said. "You were Godzilla in a skirt, tearing up anything you got your hands on."

"I wasn't tearing things up!" Shelly said. "I was researching."

"That's what you're calling it?" Terry asked. "I don't remember you putting anything back together."

"That wasn't my strength," Shelly replied.

Bryce stood then stretched. "Well, the kids should be asleep by now. I'm calling it a night. See y'all in the morning."

"I think I'll hit the bed too," Terry said.

"Make sure you get some sleep," Shelly said.

"Stay out my business, woman," Terry said with a smile.

"Guess I'll crash, too. This housecoat is failing me."

"Y'all go ahead," Bryce said. "I need to put out this fire. Love y'all."

"Me too," Shelly said.

"Me too," Terry repeated.

Bryce watched his sisters go inside then grabbed a bucket to get sand to put out the fire. Despite it all, he was blessed to have the family he had. It was something he would never take for granted.

-19-

Christmas Eve began with a warm drizzle lasting just long enough to wet the pavement. The day and the festivities the night before made for a late morning for everyone. The children woke Bryce, complaining about being hungry. He trudged into the kitchen expecting someone to be there but it was empty.

"Guess it's on me," he said.

He made coffee, then turned on the oven to make biscuits and the stove for bacon. He was sitting down with a cup of coffee when Laura entered the room.

"Boy, what you doing up so early?"

"It's 8:30 am, Mama," Bryce replied.

"Is it? That's why we don't go out anymore," Laura said.

"You're retired," Bryce replied. "You can get up whenever you want to."

Laura shook her head as she ambled to the coffee pot.

"No, you got to keep active," she said. "You start slowing down and your body shuts down. Figures it ain't got nothing else to do, so it doesn't."

"Did the doctor tell you that?" Bryce asked.

"Yes, but it's common sense." Laura made her coffee then went to the oven.

"You making biscuits?"

"Yes ma'am," Bryce said. "Bacon and eggs, too. Is that alright with you?"

"Anything's alright as long as I don't have to cook it."

Shelly slow walked into the kitchen, rubbing her eyes. "Hey, Brother. Hey, Mama."

She sat at the island then laid her head on the granite.

"If you're that sleepy you need to go back to bed," Laura commented.

"Can't," Shelly said. "Too much to do. It's Christmas Eve."

"What else do you have to do?" Bryce asked. "The tree is decorated, the presents are wrapped . . . we're good to go."

"Got some last-minute shopping I plan on doing, and y'all can't come," she said.

"Well, try to be back by noon," Bryce said. "I want to take the kids to Harbor Cove and run some of that energy out of them so they'll sleep tonight."

"There you go again," Shelly said.

"You remember how we were on Christmas Eve?" Bryce asked.

"I sure do," Laura said. "Used to take y'all forever to go to sleep. Shelly, you were the worst."

"I wanted to be the first to see the presents," she said. "And I wanted to catch Santa Claus in the act."

"You almost did one Christmas," Laura said. "Your daddy was outside on the front porch for two hours waiting for you to go back to sleep."

"Keep it down," Bryce said. "We got two believers in the next room."

As if on cue the children stormed into the kitchen.

"There they are!" Laura said. "Come hug Grandma's neck."

The children ran to Laura and gave her a hug.

"Don't forget about me!" Shelly said.

They hugged her then ran to Bryce. He kissed them both.

"Y'all go sit down while I fix your plates," he said. The children scrambled into their chairs.

"Good morning!"

Terry and João ambled into the kitchen. Terry kissed the kids on their heads then sat beside Laura. João joined Bryce at the counter.

"Biscuits and fixings," he said. "Simple and savory."

"Don't expect anything special from me," Bryce warned. "Whatever they put in the can is what they'll taste like. I'll leave the spicing to you."

João shrugged. "I guess I can stand at least one bad meal this vacation."

Bryce swung at João as he jumped away laughing.

"Come get your boyfriend before I knock him out," Bryce said.

"This is a special moment," Terry said. "My brother has threatened you. You are officially family."

"He threatened Damian yesterday," Shelly said.

Terry and Shelly did a high five.

"So y'all comedians now," Bryce said. "Bring your funny behinds over here and fix your own plates then."

Stanley and Damian entered the kitchen.

"Morning, everybody!" Stanley said.

Damian nodded his head then went to Shelly, giving her a kiss on the cheek.

"Morning," he said.

Shelly hugged him with one hand, the other holding her plate.

"Morning. You sleep well?"

"As well as I could alone."

She swatted his arm. "Don't talk so loud."

"No use in y'all whispering," Laura said. "Y'all grown."

"Does that mean we can share a room?" Shelly asked.

"No," Laura and Stanley said together.

"What about Terry and João?" Shelly asked.

"Those two have been together for five years," Laura said. "You just met this man." She looked at Damian. "No offense."

A Palmetto Christmas

"None taken," Damian replied. "I have no problem respecting your wishes, Mr. and Mrs. Jacobs."

"You're supposed to be on my side," Shelly said.

"Not with this one," Damian said. He bit into his biscuit and grinned.

"Coward," Shelly replied.

The grey clouds dissipated as they enjoyed a lively breakfast. Afterward, they washed up and went to the beach. The sun appeared, spreading light and warmth along the shore. João found an old soccer ball in the guest storage shed, so they played on the hardpacked sand. He showed off his skills, but Damian wasn't too shabby. The children flittered back and forth, kicking the ball anywhere they wanted and keeping the game from becoming too serious. Laura and Stanley took their morning stroll, Laura gathering seashells while Stanley dutifully held the sand bucket. By the time they made their way back up the beach the game was over. The children and the grandchildren sat on the sand, looking out into the ocean. Laura and Stanley sat with them.

"I'm so glad we came," Terry said. "This has been so wonderful. This year really feels like Christmas."

"Yes," João agreed.

"I'm so happy to hear you say that," Stanley replied. "Seeing y'all and the grandbabies has lifted our spirits."

"Amen," Laura said.

"We should do this every year," Shelly said. "This should be the one vacation we make a point to make." She looked at Damian and they shared a smile.

"I don't know if the children will be able to come every year," Bryce admitted. "But I'll be here, no matter what."

"And we'll meet at this house," Laura said. "We'll make sure of it."

"We'll pitch in," Terry said. "You and Daddy shouldn't have to pay for this alone."

"Now that's what I'm talking about!" Stanley said.

"And it's about time, too. Maybe y'all can start paying our house note, too."

"We don't have a house note," Laura said.

"Why you got to ruin everything?" Stanley replied. "I almost had them."

They shared a good laugh before ambling back to the house. After a light snack, Bryce dressed himself and the children.

"Shelly!" he called out.

"Yo!"

"Can you drop me and the kids off at Harbor Cove?"

Shelly walked into the great room with Damian.

"Sure. Anyone else gonna be there?" Shelly asked with a grin.

Bryce smirked. "Maybe."

"Come on," she said. "Damian and I have some last-minute shopping to do."

"What about the rest of y'all?" Bryce asked.

"João and I are going for a drive," Terry said. Terry winked at João and he smiled back.

"We're gonna take advantage of this good weather and drop the top on the convertible," João replied.

"Mama, Daddy, how about y'all?"

"We're staying here," Laura said. "Might do some walking later."

"Okay, we'll see y'all later."

Shelly, Damian, Bryce, and the children loaded into the SUV and were on their way. The ride to Habor Cove was short; they were barely into their conversations when they arrived. The children became excited when they saw the playground underneath the branches of a huge sprawling live oak, the same playground Bryce, Shelly, and Terry played when they were children. Shelly parked the car and Bryce let the children out.

They ran to the playground, joining the other cavorting children.

"Wow. This brings back memories," Shelly said. "Remember how Terry used to try to climb to the top of the tree?"

"Yeah. I remember when she almost made it, then was afraid to come down. Daddy had to climb up to get her. He was so mad!"

"I remember that!" Shelly said. "I'm tempted to try right now."

"Damian, please take her away," Bryce said.

Damian grabbed her hand. "Come on, baby. Let's go."

Shelly wrapped her arm around his waist.

"What time should I come pick you up?"

"About four," Bryce said. "We're going to hang here for a minute then ride to South Beach Marina for lunch. I hope they still have that ice cream shop."

"Google is your friend," Shelly said.

A black convertible Beetle pulled into the parking lot beside the SUV. The door opened and India emerged, a wide smile on her face. She wore form-fitting slacks and a sweater, her braids covered by a mud print wrap.

"That woman is not dressed for playing, at least not with kids."

Bryce couldn't argue.

"Well, I guess it's time for us to go," Shelly said.

"Y'all don't have to," Bryce replied.

"We do. Besides, I don't want to intrude on your family time."

Bryce looked at Damian. "Get out while you can."

Damian laughed. "I'm in for the long haul."

Bryce shook his head. "Don't say I didn't warn you."

Shelly turned her attention to India.

"Hey, girl! Thank you so much for last night!"

They hugged.

"You're welcome," India replied. "I had a good time. And my uncle can't stop talking about João. He's a big fan."

"João is full of surprises," Shelly said. "I wouldn't be surprised if he performed open heart surgery. Terry did good. She better be glad she met him first."

"I know that's right," India replied.

"Hey, I'm standing right here," Damian said.

Shelly sashayed over to Damian and kissed him.

"Yes, you are."

She hugged Bryce. "We gotta go. Pick y'all up at four?"

"Yep. See y'all later."

Shelly and Damian left. Bryce grasped India's hands briefly and they shared a smile.

"I'm glad you could make it," he said.

"I woke up early and baked a cake so I could be here," India replied. "You owe me a good time."

"And a good time you shall have," Bryce said.

"Miss India!" Constance shouted.

"Hi, Constance!"

Constance grinned. "Chase me!"

Bryce laughed. "See, the party's about to start."

To Bryce's surprise, India sprinted toward Constance. Constance squealed and ran. Bryce ambled to the playground and grabbed Cameron, carrying him to the swings. After a few more minutes on the playground, they rented tandem bikes then cycled the meandering bike trail from Harbor Cove to South Marina. The paved path wove through stately neighborhoods and forests, crossing bridges over tidal creeks and marshland. This had always been Bryce's favorite part of their vacation and he was finally experiencing it with his children . . . and India. Their time together in the past never went beyond the ocean, but now he was enjoying the island beyond their childhood confines. It was a good thing, but then again it wasn't.

They reached their destination just before his thoughts crashed his mood. South Marina was different from Harbor Cove. While the cove bustled with tourists, upscale shops, and huge yachts, the Marina exuded a more laidback vibe. The bleach-white wooden buildings seemed more like a village. The small two-story buildings held small souvenir shops and clothing stores, while the only restaurant possessed a large dining patio overlooking the small harbor and nearby marsh. The aroma of freshly cooked seafood stirred Bryce's hunger as they rode to the bike racks. Bryce secured the bikes and they walked to the restaurant.

"Let's eat outside, Daddy!" Cameron asked. "I want to feed the birds!"

"I don't think everyone wants seagulls flying over their tables dropping little packages," Bryce said.

"You're so nasty, Daddy!" Constance said.

"Yes he is," India agreed.

"We'll eat outside, but no feeding the birds, okay?"

Cameron pouted. "Okay."

They sat down to a meal of fried shrimp and fries for the kids and shrimp and grits for Bryce. India had the snapper and fried oysters. After the meal, they went to the ice cream shop for brownies and vanilla ice cream.

India rubbed her stomach.

"I haven't eaten this much in a long time. And tomorrow is Christmas!"

Bryce nodded. "It's that time of year. At least we'll work off a little on the way back."

"I hope so."

"Hey, I got something to show y'all," Bryce said. "Follow me."

They left the retail area, walking down the sidewalk among the nearby condos. After a few blocks, they came across a gap between the buildings filled with grass and trees. A sandy path sliced between the foliage. Bryce smiled.

"It's still here. I thought they would have built something here by now."

He looked back, taking the kids hands.

"Come on!"

They ran down the path which ended at a narrow deserted beach.

"A hidden gem," India said.

"Something like that," Bryce replied. "Me and Daddy wandered off one day while Mama, Terry and Shelly were shopping and we found this. There wasn't a lot of people, but there were dolphins everywhere. They were even swimming along the shore. I remember Daddy saying, 'We spent all that money to see dolphins and all we had to do was come here!'"

"There are better places to see them," India said. "We locals know where they are, but we don't tell. Next thing you know they'll be condos everywhere and gates keeping us from getting to them."

"I understand," Bryce said.

"Daddy, look!" Constance shouted. She jumped up and down, pointing into the surf.

"I saw a dolphin!"

"A dolphin!" Cameron repeated.

They scanned the waters and a minute later a familiar dorsal fin rose over the surface. More fins appeared, joining the solitary dolphin.

"See?" Bryce said.

They sat on the sand, watching the dolphins for almost an hour. A few swam so close their entire bodies were exposed. The children hurried down, following the pod along the shore. Bryce and India followed them, their hands finding each other. After a few moments, India let go.

"Bryce, what are we doing?"

"Enjoying the day," Bryce replied.

"You know what I mean. I feel like we're playing house."

"I just wanted to spend some time with you," Bryce said. "I wasn't sure you were going to show up."

"I wasn't either," India said. "We haven't seen each other since we were teenagers. I wasn't sure I was going to like grown up you. But I do. A lot. And that's kind of a problem. You have so much going on in your life, on top of the fact we live in two different cities."

"I glad I'm not the only one thinking so hard," Bryce confessed. "You're right. My life is a mess right now. And even when I get things sorted out, it's still going to be a challenge. But I'm not gonna lie. I'm hoping you're willing to try."

"I don't know," India said.

Bryce's phone buzzed. It was a message from Shelly.

"We're here. Where are you?"

"Wow. I didn't realize it was so late. We have to get back."

He texted Shelly.

"Give us a few. We're at South Marina."
"We can come pick you up."
"Nah. We rode bikes."
"Cool! We'll do some window shopping until y'all get here."

They left the beach, the children waving goodbye to the dolphins. The bike ride back was more leisurely, Bryce taking in the sights along the way, the children barely pedaling with their tired legs. They reached Harbor Cove as the children complained. Bryce turned in the bikes, and he and India carried the kids to the SUV. Shelly and Damian showed up moments later.

"I see your diabolical plan worked," Shelly said as she took Cameron from India.

"Not exactly," Bryce said. "I didn't want them to go to sleep this soon."

They put the children into their car seats. Shelly and Damian climbed into the SUV.

"Give me a minute," Bryce said. "I'm gonna walk India to her car."

"Always the gentleman," India said as he approached. They strolled to her car.

"I probably won't see you tomorrow," Bryce said.

"Probably not," India replied. "I'm leaving on the 26th. Flying to New York."

They kissed. Bryce didn't care if the children saw them; this was something he needed to do.

"Don't lose my number," Bryce said.

"Are you sure?" India asked.

"I'm sure. I know what I want. I hope you want it, too."

India sighed. "I'll tell you what. If you still think this will work after you get back to Chicago, send me a text. You have a whole 'nother situation waiting for you there, and she doesn't want to let go. You need to be sure you want to. I don't want to be a rebound chick. I'm not going to be. If you want us to try at being together, you need to be free and clear of everything and everyone else."

Bryce nodded. "You'll hear from me."

India smiled then kissed his cheek.

"Goodbye, Bryce Jacobs."

"Goodbye, India Stewart."

India climbed into her car, let the top down, then drove away. Bryce watched until her car disappeared around a curve. He walked back to the SUV.

"Well?" Shelly asked.
Bryce shrugged. "I don't know."
Shelly smiled. "That's better than a no. Let's get back to the house. Christmas is almost here!"

-20-

The fire crackled on the patio, the constant hum of the ocean a soothing background. Stanley and Laura sat side by side holding hands, watching the sunlight diminish, the watery horizon slowly melding into the darkening sky. Inside, the children cleaned up after dinner while the grandchildren hovered around the Christmas tree, attempting to figure out what was in each wrapped gift. Laura closed her eyes then smiled.

"Remember the first time we came here?" she asked.

"Mmm hmm," Stanley answered. "We got that advertisement about time shares. That was when they used to let you stay in the condos. We took so many vacations that way."

Laura chuckled. "Those sales pitches were so annoying. But they were worth it."

"It was my first time to the beach," Stanley said.

"I can't believe it took you so long," Laura replied.

Stanley shrugged. "Never thought about going until I met you. You made it sound so peaceful. You were right."

"We should have bought that condo," Laura said. "I bet that thing is worth a million dollars now."

"Probably," Stanley replied. "Too late now. But it's all good. I think I'd rather visit than live here. Keeps it special."

"I don't know about that," Laura said. "I wouldn't mind being able to walk to the beach every day."

"That would be nice." Stanley squeezed Laura's hand.

"What you thinking about now?" Laura asked.

"The first time we met."

Laura felt a warm rush over her cheeks.

"You would."

"How could I forget? You came walking in wearing them hot pants and halter top. Cutest belly button I'd ever seen."

"Like you were looking at my belly button," Laura said.

Stanley laughed. "And that 'fro?"

"I did have a nice 'fro. And I was fine, too."

"Still are," Stanley said.

Laura gave Stanley a side eye. "You weren't too bad looking yourself."

"I know," Stanley said. "We Jacobs men are cut like that. Look at Bryce."

"Don't go getting the big head. You wasn't the only boy I had my eye on. You just happened to be the nicest. And the funniest."

"I'm glad I was. Otherwise we wouldn't be here."

Stanley stood and tossed another log on the fire. He sat as fast as his knees allowed, then let out a grunt before taking Laura's hand again.

"I have to admit, I got nervous when you went off to college. I figured one of those college boys was going to blow your mind."

Laura laughed. "Blow my mind? I ain't heard anybody say that in forever. And you know that wasn't going to happen. You'd already done it. All I could think of was getting back home on the weekends and holidays to see you. Then you up and joined the Army."

"Yeah that wasn't the best idea," Stanley said. "But it all worked out."

"Yes it did. Here we are with three wonderful children, two grandkids and a whole lot of love. Can't ask for more than that."

"No, we can't."

Bryce came out of the house, sat hard then let out a breath.

"The kids are officially asleep," he said.

"You sure?" Laura asked.

"No, but at least they're in the bed. It'll probably be another hour before they go to sleep. They're listening to their Charlie Brown Christmas CD."

"Listening to a CD?" Laura stood up. "Let me go read my babies a story!"

Laura hurried into the house. Bryce took her chair.

"How you feeling, Son?" Stanley asked.

"Good," Bryce replied. "I'm glad we came down. Just the thing we needed."

"Happy to hear that," Stanley said. "Me and your mama were talking about how good it was to have everybody together."

"Even without April?" Bryce asked. "I know how much y'all like her."

"Liked her," Stanley corrected. "Y'all always come first. When she hurt you, she hurts us. I don't wish bad on her, but I'm not concerned about her future. Unless it's with you."

Bryce rubbed his forehead. "I should hate her for what she did, but I don't. I don't understand why."

"Because love is always trying to heal wounds," Stanley replied. "It's always trying to find ways to keep on going, even when it makes no sense. You loved April hard. That kind of love takes time to fade."

"I'm not sure it ever will," Bryce said.

"Ain't nothing wrong with that either," Stanley replied. "You can still love a person but move on."

Bryce looked at Stanley. "You sound like you're speaking from experience."

"Shoot no," Stanley said. "Your mama was the first woman I fell in love with, and I married her. I was watching a daytime talk show a few weeks ago and they were talking about it."

Bryce laughed. "Okay then. I'll take their advice."

A PALMETTO CHRISTMAS

Shelly and Damian came to the patio with two bottles of wine and glasses.

"So this is where y'all are," Shelly said. "Where's Mama?"

"Reading Cameron and Constance to sleep," Bryce said.

"I hope it doesn't take long," Shelly said. "This wine needs drinking."

"You know I'm not much of a wine drinker," Stanley said.

"You'll like this one," Shelly replied. "I looked all over for it just for you. And if you don't, you can act like it for my sake."

Stanley laughed. "Alright, Baby Girl."

João and Terry joined them. Terry's eyes went wide when she saw the wine bottles.

"Wow little sister. Somebody spent some money."

"Only the best for the best, big sister."

"I'm tempted to throw something together to eat with it," João said.

"No time for that," Shelly said. "Just wanted to have a drink together to remember the moment."

Laura returned to the patio.

"What's this?"

"A Christmas Eve toast," Shelly said. Damian opened the wine bottles while Shelly passed out the glasses.

"So this is what you were doing all day? Looking for wine?" Laura said.

"Yes," Shelly replied. "It had to be the right one."

She filled everyone's glasses, then hers and Damian.

"Mama, Daddy, I know this wasn't the vacation y'all imagined, but we'd like to thank you for tolerating us. I think I speak for everyone when I say this is one of the best times we've spent together. We didn't do much, but what we did, we did together. Cheers!"

They raised their glasses and sipped. Stanley's eyebrows rose. "This is good wine!"

"Told you," Shelly replied.

Damian stepped forward. "I'd like to say something, if you don't mind."

"Not at all," Laura said.

"I just want to thank you all for being so welcoming. I was surprised when Shelly invited me. We knew each other, but I wasn't sure we knew each other well enough to be visiting family. I kept thinking, 'what if her family hates me?' But now I know why she asked me. It was so we could get to know each other better in a place where she felt comfortable. I'm glad I came."

"We're glad you came, too," Stanley said. "You're a good man, the kind of man Shelly deserves. I hope she doesn't mess it up."

"Daddy!"

Stanley laughed. "I'm just messing with you, baby."

"I'm glad we came, too," Terry said. "I mean, it's not São Paulo, but it'll do."

Everyone laughed.

"Seriously though, I've been away too long for the wrong reasons," Terry continued. "I didn't realize how much I missed you all until the moment we arrived. Sea Island holds special meaning for us, and to come together here was perfect. And I'm happy that you finally got to meet João, and that he loves me and I love him, too."

Terry and João kissed.

"I don't have much to say," João said. "I know now why Terry is such an extraordinary person after meeting all of you. It was the one piece that was missing, and now I feel like our relationship is complete."

He raised his glass and everyone took another sip.

Bryce stepped up.

A PALMETTO CHRISTMAS

"Well, y'all know my situation," he said. "Things are in flux for me personally and professionally. Being here has given me time to reflect without the pressures of the city. Sea Island has always been a salve for me, even when I was a boy. I still haven't figured everything out, but knowing that I have a family that loves me and will be here for me makes everything easier to deal with."

"What about you, Daddy?"

"I'll let your mama speak for us," Stanley said. "We don't agree on everything, but the one thing we do see eye to eye on is how we feel about y'all."

Laura took a sip of wine.

"I can't say how happy I am to have all my babies together," Laura said. "I understand everyone is grown and have their own lives, but us coming together like this will always be the highlight for me and your daddy. Damian, João, I'm glad y'all were able to join us. I'm glad to see my daughters happy. I hope it continues."

Laura raised her glass and they took another sip. Stanley finished his wine then sat the glass down.

"Well, I don't know about the rest of y'all, but I'm going to get some sleep. See y'all Christmas morning!"

Laura finished her glass. "If Stanley's going to bed, I am, too. Can't let him get a head start on me or I'll be dealing with his snoring all night."

"I don't snore," Stanley said. "I've never heard it."

"Of course you haven't. That's why I do."

"Come on then," Stanley said. "I might fall asleep before we get to the room."

Stanley and Laura retired to their rooms. Shelly, Damian, Terry, João, and Bryce finished the wine. Bryce stood then stretched.

"I'm turning in," Bryce said. "The children will be the first up and I'll be with them. Goodnight, y'all."

"We're out too," Terry said. She took João's hand and they went inside.

Shelly and Damian sat down, the fire whittled down to embers.

"This was a good idea," Shelly said.

"It was," Damian replied. "You're so giving."

"It's my family," she replied. "I'd do anything for them."

She kissed Damian's cheek.

"Come on. Let's go to bed."

"I wish we could," Damian said.

"You could come visit," Shelly said.

"Just for a few minutes," Damian said.

"Just a few," Shelly agreed.

They put out the fire, took each other's hand, then went inside.

A PALMETTO CHRISTMAS

-21-

"Daddy! Daddy! It's Christmas!"

Bryce stretched and opened his eyes just in time to see Cameron and Constance run out of the room. The wine had him groggy, so he struggled into his housecoat and staggered into the family room. Mama and Daddy had left some of the children's presents unwrapped and the little ones went straight to them. After doing a tour with them, Bryce stole away to make a pot of coffee.

"Merry Christmas!"

Laura and Stanley strolled into the room, a surprised look on their faces.

"Has Santa Claus been here?" Laura said.

"Yes!" Both children shouted.

Constance grabbed their hands and pulled.

"Come see!"

By the time they could break away, the coffee was made. Bryce poured them a cup.

"Merry Christmas," he said.

Merry Christmas baby," Laura said.

Merry Christmas son," Stanley said.

Bryce watched Cameron and Constance play as he sipped his coffee. His phone buzzed and he answered.

"Merry Christmas!" April said.

"Merry Christmas," he replied. "You're up early."

"I wanted to speak to the babies," she said. "How are you doing?"

"I'm good. You?"

"Other than sitting in my apartment by myself, I'm doing okay."

Bryce shook his head.

"Cameron! Constance! Mommy's on the phone."

The children dropped their toys and ran over. Bryce put the phone on speaker then placed it on the table. He walked away into the family room, joining Laura and Stanley.

"You okay?" Laura asked.

"I'm fine," Bryce replied. "It's Christmas and I'm home."

"Merry Christmas!"

Shelly and Damian entered the room wearing red onesies decorated with Santa heads and elf hats. Laura and Stanley laughed out loud while Bryce shook his head.

"So this is what you were shopping for yesterday?" Bryce said.

Shelly grinned. "Yes, sir!"

They sat in front of the tree and began separating presents by name. João and Terry strolled into the family room.

"Merry Christmas," Terry said.

"Feliz Natal!" João said.

They passed through to the kitchen, making cups of coffee then returning to sit with everyone while Shelly and Damian finished giving out gifts.

"Let's see what we got!"

They opened their presents with childlike enthusiasm. Cameron and Constance came back, and Constance handed Bryce his phone. The children hovered beside him, announcing each of his gifts. Laura and Stanley smiled over what they received, each item a sentimental reminder of their children now grown. Shelly laughed at the gag gifts she received from Terry and Bryce; Bryce and Terry were surprised at the thoughtful choices Shelly had made. Damian was very emotional as he opened his gifts, dropping his reserved demeanor and hugging everyone. João was his exuberant self, laughing loudly with each gift revealed.

A Palmetto Christmas

"Mama and Daddy, João and I got you something special," Terry said.

Terry nodded at João and he trotted back to their room. He returned with a large square package.

"I know what this is!" Laura said.

"Merry Christmas, Mr. and Mrs. Jacobs." João sat the package before Laura and Stanley. Laura tore into the paper then squealed. She picked up the painting, showing it to everyone then handed it off to Stanley before wrapping Terry and João into a hug.

"Thank y'all so much! It's beautiful!"

"Sure is," Stanley said. "Now we just need one of your paintings."

"Yes we do," Laura agreed.

Terry's eyes glistened. "Of course, of course!"

It was her turn to hug her parents.

Once all the presents had been opened, Stanley began gathering wrapping paper as the others started for the kitchen for breakfast.

"Wait," João said.

He held a small box wrapped with golden foil and topped with a red bow.

"It seems we forgot one."

Shelly looked puzzled. "I don't remember that one. Who is it for?"

"It doesn't say," João replied. "I'll open it."

João sat next to Terry then unwrapped the present, revealing a plain white box. He opened the box; inside was a blue jewelry box. João looked at Terry and winked. Terry jumped to her feet, her hands covering her mouth. João took out the box then dropped to one knee in front of Terry.

"Ayeee!" Shelly shouted.

João looked into Terry's eyes.

"From the day I first met you, I knew you were the one. I decided that day I would spend the rest of my life convincing you the same. I bought this ring a year after we began dating, wishing for the moment I would get to present it to you. I can't think of any better day than today."

Terry's eyes glistened.

João opened the box then took out the diamond engagement ring. "Terry Jacobs, will you marry me?"

Terry stood frozen. Just a few days ago she's found enough courage to tell João she loved him. Now he knelt before her, asking her to spend the rest of her life with him. She lowered her hands and smiled. This was right. It was time. She nodded her head.

"Tell him, girl!" Shelly said.

"Yes," Terry replied. "Yes, yes, yes!"

Terry extended her hand and João put the ring on her finger. She fell into his waiting arms and they kissed.

"Now that's a Christmas present," Laura said.

Terry and João stood and were surrounded by the family.

"Welcome to the family," Stanley said.

"Alright now, future brother-in-law," Bryce said.

Shelly hugged them both, jumping up and down.

Laura sat down, closed her eyes, and said a prayer. She stood then grinned.

"So who's ready for breakfast?"

The family filed into the kitchen, leaving João and Terry alone.

"I don't know what to say," Terry said.

"You already said enough," João replied. "You said yes."

"How did you know I would?" Terry asked.

"I didn't," João replied. "When you told me you loved me I figured it was now or never."

"What if I had said no?"

"You didn't. That's all that matters. So when and where?"

"Here. Next spring."

João eyes widened. "Wow. That was quick!"

"We've been together for five years. No reason to wait. And I don't want an elaborate wedding. Just close friends and family. Oh wait, what about your family?"

"I called them last night and told them I was going to ask you. I'm happy I can call them back and share the good news. We'll fly them in. They'll love Sea Island."

"Then there's nothing left to say," Terry said.

"Except I do," João replied.

They kissed again.

"I love you so much," Terry said.

"I love you too," João replied.

* * *

Breakfast went by fast. The children resumed their playing while the grownups lounged about, Laura's Christmas songs playing in the background. Shelly was admiring Terry's engagement ring when she heard Damian clear his throat.

"What's up, Damian?" Bryce asked.

"Shelly, can I speak to you for a minute?"

Shelly's face went serious. "You better not be about to propose!"

Damian laughed. "No, it's not that. I need your help with something."

"Go on, girl," Terry said. "Me and this rock ain't going nowhere."

Shelly followed Damian onto the patio.

"I'm gonna call my dad, and I want you to be with me," he said.

Shelly hugged him. "That's wonderful!"

Damian shrugged. "We'll see. He might not answer."

"You won't know until you call."

Damian took a deep breath then punched in the numbers. He put the phone on speaker then waited. It rang for a long while before someone answered.

"Hello?"
"Dad?"
"Who is this?"
"It's Damian."
"Damian?"
"Yeah Dad, it's me."

There was a long silence.

"Dad?"
"Son? Oh my God. It's so great to hear your voice!"

Damian put his hand over his mouth, his eyes glistening.
"It's alright," Shelly whispered. "It's alright."

"Son? You still there?"
"Yeah Dad. I'm still here."
"How are you? Is everything okay?"
Damian grinned. "Everything is fine, Dad. I just wanted to wish you a Merry Christmas."
"It is now! Where are you? Germany?"
"No, I'm actually in the States. In South Carolina."
"That's wonderful. I'm glad you were able to make it back. Who was that I heard in the background?"
"My girlfriend, Shelly. We're spending the holiday with her family on Sea Island."
"Shelly. I like that. Is she as pretty as her name?"
Damian smiled at Shelly. "I think so."
"That's great. It's good you're not alone on the holidays."
Damian hesitated.

A PALMETTO CHRISTMAS

"Dad, since I'm in the States, I was thinking about visiting."

"Are you sure that's what you want to do?"

"Yes, Dad. I want to. It's been too long."

"You have no idea how long I've been waiting to hear you say that. Son, I wasn't fair to you. I took you for granted. I know I can't make up for the past, but I'd love to set things right for the future."

"We'll talk about that when I get there," Damian said. "I have to go. Merry Christmas, Dad."

"Merry Christmas, son. I love you."

Damian looked stunned. Shelly touched his cheek.

"Only say it if you mean it," she whispered. Damian nodded.

"Love you too, Dad."

Damian hung up. He hugged Shelly.

"I couldn't have done this without you." He drew back. "Are you okay going with me?"

"Yes," Shelly replied. "Family is everything."

"It may not work out," Damian admitted. "I don't know how I'm going to act when I see him face-to-face."

"At least you're trying," Shelly said. "If it turns sour we'll walk away."

"You make it sound easy," Damian said.

"It won't be. That's why I'll be there. I'll always be there. As long as you want me to be." Shelly kissed his cheek. "Let's get back inside. We're missing all the fun."

As they entered the house everyone was running from the kitchen. Laura was behind them, waving a towel.

"Everybody out except the cooks!" she said. "Time to make Christmas dinner."

Her eyes fell on Shelly.

"Come on, baby girl."

Shelly saluted then kissed Damian's cheek.

"See you on the other side."

Laura followed Shelly into the kitchen with her eyes.

227

"I volunteer!" João announced.

Laura laughed. "I was about to get you next."

João strode into the kitchen.

"It's an honor and a privilege."

"Famous last words," Shelly said. "You ain't never cooked with my mama on Christmas."

"Based on today, I should get used to it," João replied.

"Yes you should, bruh-in-law," Bryce said.

Stanley sat on the sofa, stretching his arms before folding them behind his head. "I guess that means I'm off the hook."

"No it doesn't," Laura replied. "The dishes still need washing."

"What you need me for?" Stanley said. "You got them."

"Come on, Daddy. I got your back," Terry said.

Stanley smiled at her. "This is why you're my favorite."

"I thought I was your favorite," Bryce said.

"You gonna help do the dishes?" Stanley asked.

"I have to watch the kids," Bryce replied.

"Well, there you go," Stanley said with a wink.

The house was filled with smells of Christmas. The aroma of roasting turkey permeated every room, while the buzzing of the mixer underscored the holiday music wafting from the small speakers. Despite their energy, the children fell asleep in the family room while the grownups talked, joked, and drank.

Dinner was ready late afternoon. It was a spread just like home in Atlanta; roasted turkey with extra turkey legs, collard greens prepared the day before, sweet potato casserole, macaroni and cheese, and Janine's red rice. Everyone retired to their rooms to wash up, while Bryce woke up the children. They met at the dining room table, where Stanley said grace.

A PALMETTO CHRISTMAS

"Since we're on vacation y'all can eat where you want," Laura said.

Everyone gathered at the table. The joy that emanated there was too strong to resist. Laura and Stanley took a pause, watching their children and grandchildren enjoy their meals and they grasped hands under the table.

"We did this," Laura said.

"Yes we did," Stanley replied. "Best thing that ever happened to us."

Laura kissed Stanley's cheek. "Merry Christmas, baby."

Stanley kissed her back.

"Merry Christmas."

The doorbell rang. Laura looked at the door her face scrunched up.

"Who would be visiting on Christmas?"

"I'll get it," Bryce said.

He stood and the children did, too.

"Finish your dinner," Bryce said.

Bryce strolled to the door then peered through the peephole. He smiled and opened the door. Janine stood on the porch with India. Janine held a cake plate. India held a large present.

"Merry Christmas!" they said.

"Is that Janine?" Laura called out.

"Yes, it is!" Janine called back.

"Come on in, girl," Laura said.

Bryce and India lingered at the door.

"This is a pleasant surprise," Bryce said.

"Auntie Janine asked me to help her," India replied.

"I'm glad she did. I didn't know Miss Janine was your aunt."

"You never asked."

"Why would I?" Bryce's eyes widened. "That explains it!"

229

India laughed. "So you finally figured it out. The first time I saw you was at her restaurant with your family. That's how I always knew you were on the island."

"Y'all come on in!" Laura called out.

India and Bryce walked into the kitchen together.

"I made y'all something and bought you a present for helping out with the meals," Janine said. "We've never had so much help, and never had so many meals to give out. It was wonderful."

"Don't mention it," Laura said. "What you got in that cake plate?"

Janine took off the lid, revealing a sweet potato pie.

"Christmas dinner is officially complete!" Laura said.

Janine took the gift from India and presented it to Laura.

"Got you this too as a token of our appreciation."

"You didn't have to!" Laura said.

"But I did. Now open it."

Everyone gathered around the table as Laura opened the present. She lifted the tissue paper then gasped.

"Oh my goodness!"

Laura lifted a seagrass basket from the box. The size and intricate design were the result of master-level skilled hands. Laura shook her head.

"No, no, Janine. Take this back. It's too expensive."

"You don't like it?" Janine asked.

"Of course I do! It's beautiful! But whatever we did for you wasn't worth this much."

"Now Laura, you know how cheap I am," Janine said. "Ain't no way I would have bought you something like this. My sister Darlene up in Mt. Pleasant made this. I told her what y'all did for us, and she sent it down as a gift."

"That is amazing," Stanley said.

"Sure is," Shelly agreed.

"Well in that case, I'll keep it," Laura said. She gave Janine a warm hug.

"Now that that's done, let's eat some pie!" Janine said.

Laura and Janine cut and handed out pie slices to everyone before serving themselves. Bryce sat in the family room watching the children play. India came over and sat beside him.

"So when are you flying back?" India asked.

"Tomorrow. You're leaving tomorrow too, right?"

"Yes." Bryce detected a bit of sadness in her voice. He felt the same but managed to keep smiling.

"I hope y'all have fun in New York," he said.

"We definitely will." India ate a portion of her pie piece. "Wow! This is good."

Bryce tasted his and nodded in agreement.

"So what are your New Year's Eve plans?" India asked.

"I'm spending a quiet evening alone," Bryce said. "The children will be with April."

"That sounds lonely," India replied. "Don't you have a crew to hang with?"

Bryce chuckled. "I gave that up when I married April. She insisted on it. My time was her time."

"That sounds . . . fun."

"It wasn't her fault," Bryce said. "I agreed to it. I wanted her to be happy, and I was willing to do anything to make it happen."

"Well, if you get bored you can fly to New York and hand out with me and my crew."

Bryce laughed. "Yeah, right."

"I'm serious," India replied. "I can't stand the thought of you spending New Year's Eve alone."

"It won't be the first time," Bryce said. "And what would your girls think about me busting up in y'all space?"

"They'd be fine," India replied. "All you have to do is get a ticket. You have a place to stay."

Bryce was about to laugh when he noticed India's serious expression.

"Ah . . . I'll think about it?" he finally said.

India grinned. "You do that."

She winked as she stood with her plate then walked over to Shelly and Terry. Terry flashed her engagement ring and India shouted in surprise. Bryce watched her with his sisters. She was so natural with them, unlike April. April tolerated Shelly and Terry; India embraced them.

"Daddy! Hurry up! We want to play!"

Constance stood before him, her little arms folded across her chest, her right foot tapping the floor. Bryce picked up the rest of his pie and stuffed it in his mouth. Constance laughed as he chewed.

"Finished!" he said. He jumped out of his seat and chased her around the room, Cameron running behind him.

The day moved on as everyone settled down. Janine and India said their goodbyes after a few slices of pie. Laura, Stanley, Shelly, and Damian relaxed around the television while Terry, João, Bryce, and the children spent the rest of the day on the beach until the fading sunlight and chill forced them inside. Dinner was seconds from the earlier meal, leaving everyone full and sleepy.

"This has been a day!" Laura declared.

"Yes it has," Stanley said. "I'm going to bed."

"Shelly, you leaving tomorrow?" Laura asked.

"Yes ma'am," Shelly replied.

"How about you, Terry?"

"João and I are going to spend a few days in Savannah then head back."

"Bryce?"

"Tomorrow. Got to get the kids to April."
"So I guess this is it," Stanley said.
"Don't make it sound so final," Laura fussed. "This is it for now. We got any more of that firewood left?"
"I think so," Bryce said.
"Y'all go get your coats," Laura said. "We have marshmallows and hot chocolate, and it's finally cold enough. Meet y'all at the fire pit!"
Bryce and Damian built the fire, while Laura and João made hot chocolate. The family gathered around the flames, using driftwood sticks for skewers. Laura served the hot chocolate, and they talked and joked until the children and Stanley were fast asleep. Bryce and Shelly carried the children inside and put them to bed; Laura woke Stanley and guided him to their room. By the time Bryce returned to put out the fire, everyone had retired to their rooms. He took a seat and watched the fire burn down to embers as he thought of the past few days on the island.
"You still awake?"
Terry carried a cup of hot chocolate then sat down.
"Yeah. Just thinking," Bryce replied.
"About what?"
"Everything."
Terry leaned over then hugged him.
"It's gonna be alright."
"You know what? I think so. I don't know what I'm going to do, or who I'm going to be with, but I know things will be okay."
"Kids meeting!"
Shelly ran to them, dropping into Bryce's lap."
Hey! You're too big for this!"
"Aw, big brother!"
She kissed him on his forehead before getting up. "This has been a great weekend! I hate going back."
"Me too," Bryce said.

"Let's promise to make this an annual thing," Terry said. "Just us kids."

"Sounds like a plan," Shelly said.

"I like it," Bryce agreed.

They did a group hug like they used to when they were children.

"The future feels better already," Terry said.

Bryce stood. "Well, I better get to bed. I have three people to get ready for the flight tomorrow. Love y'all."

"Love you too, big brother," Shelly said.

They took a long look at each other, then went inside.

-22-

Shelly looked at her watched then frowned.
"Let's go!" she shouted. "We're running late!"
Bryce showed up with the children, bags packed.
"Sorry about that," he said. "Had to do the potty thing. Where's Terry and João?"
"Right here," Terry said. João nodded good morning as he carried their bags to the car. Damian, waiting by the hatch, helped him load.
Laura and Stanley came outside, their faces sad.
"Y'all sure you can't stay for breakfast?" Laura asked.
"No, Mama," Shelly replied. "Our flight leaves in a couple of hours, and Bryce's flight an hour after that. He needs more time because of the kids."
Laura frowned. "Okay then. Y'all come give us some sugar."
Laura and Stanely hugged everyone, Laura kissing cheeks and Stanley being more selective.
"We enjoyed y'all," Stanley said. "Let's not let this be a one-time thing."
"We won't, Daddy," Shelly replied. "We're already planning the next vacation."
"And we have a wedding, too!" João said. Terry nodded.
"And it will be glorious," she added.
Everyone loaded into the SUV. Stanley took the driver's seat.
"I'll be back in a few," he said to Laura. He backed out of the driveway, onto the street then drove away, Terry and João following in their car. Laura waved, watching until the vehicles disappeared around a curve.

She was preparing breakfast when Stanley returned.

"I guess that's that," Stanley said.

"Yes it is," Laura replied. "Wasn't we planned."

"It was better," Stanley said.

"Yes, it was."

He walked to Laura and she held his hand.

"Want to go walk the beach after breakfast?"

"I figured we'd start packing," Stanley said. "We have to head out tomorrow."

"I think we should stay until after New Year's."

Stanley frowned. "We booked the house until tomorrow."

Laura grinned. "Let me handle that. You still got the renter's number?"

"I do."

"Then let's go get them extra days."

Stanley draped his arms around Laura's shoulders; Laura hugged his waist.

"You something else," Stanley said.

"Yes I am," Laura replied.

-End-

ABOUT THE AUTHOR

I'm Milton Davis, an award-winning Black Speculative fiction author, and owner of MVmedia, LLC, a publishing company specializing in Science Fiction and Fantasy based on African/African Diaspora history, culture, and traditions. I'm the author of thirty novels and short story collections and editor/coeditor of ten anthologies. *A Palmetto Christmas* is my first contemporary fiction novel. I hope you enjoyed it.

Lightning bugs on a summer evening. A lazy river swollen from spring rain. The taste of honeysuckles. The aroma of wild grapes ripe on the vine. A collection of fantasy and contemporary fiction stories set in Southwest Georgia based on the experiences of author Milton J. Davis, Muscadine Wine is a personal homage to the land and Black people of South Georgia. Available from MVmedia and anywhere books are sold.